THE PREFECT OF PANAMÁ

THE PREFECT OF PANAMÁ

First book in the series *The Agency*

ERIC L. HANEY

A POST HILL PRESS BOOK

The Prefect of Panamá

ISBN: 978-1-68261-612-3
ISBN (eBook): 978-1-68261-613-0

Cover art by Christian Bentulan
Interior design and composition by Greg Johnson, Textbook Perfect

Post Hill Press
New York • Nashville
posthillpress.com

Published in the United States of America

Dedicated to mi hija querida, Mercedes.

UNO

Yuri Kutasov was barely conscious, able to move little more than his head. His arms, legs, and waist were restrained by heavily padded leather straps that held him tethered securely to the metal railing of the hospital bed. Clear liquid from two glass IV bottles dripped slowly into each arm. A blindingly bright overhead light prevented him from seeing more than indistinct shadows.

But he could hear. In addition to the voices that seemed to be speaking to him from somewhere within the depths of his own head, he could hear a pounding—the unrelenting hammering of his own heart.

A shadow loomed above him and Yuri heard that particular voice again. The one that spoke to him in Russian. In the sweet-sounding dialect and accent of the village where he had been born and grew to young manhood. A poor farm village that existed no longer. Peasants wiped from the face of the earth by the passage of the Wehrmacht during their winter retreat out of Russia.

The voice insisted. "Yuri. Listen to me, Yuri. What is the name of the agent? The *American* agent? His name, Yuri. You remember his name?"

Yuri truly wanted to answer. He tried to mouth the words, but the task was too large. The name would not form. It would not come into focus. It danced, it flitted, it hid in the dark corners of his mind where no matter how hard he tried, it just would not take shape. In his agitation, Yuri tried to fight the name out from its hiding place. He thrashed his head wildly and arched his back with the effort, but the name refused to emerge. It just wouldn't come out! He threw his head back and screamed.

He fell slumped against the bed, gasping for breath. The heart monitor above him showed a frantic, dangerously rapid pulse and shallow rate.

The bedside shadows moved again. A second voice—this time American and not gentle—barked rapid orders, "He's almost there. He's about to give it to us. Increase the chemical levels."

A hand reached toward one of the IV bottles, but before it could obey the American and increase the dosage, a German with clipped authority interceded, commanding, "Stop! That is all for now. He has reached the limit of endurance. To go further could be dangerous, even fatal."

The American was not happy. He spoke through clenched teeth. "Doctor, we almost have what we need. This is why we're here."

The German: "For now, no more. We can proceed anew when he has had time to stabilize. He's going nowhere, and we have all the time in the world. Take him to recovery. Monitor his condition carefully."

"But Doctor—"

A second American: "Enough." This voice carried the gravitas of command that conveyed easy dismissal. "Doctor, as you order." And the interrogation was over.

The light was switched off. The IV needles were removed.

In his blackout state, Yuri heard none of this. But he felt the touch on his arms as the needles were withdrawn. And he felt the motion of the bed as it was wheeled from the room. But he knew no more until he awoke later in a dimly lit room.

Yuri lay very still, his eyes closed, unsure of his location or whether he was awake or dreaming. But then he felt a hand on his forehead; a comforting, soothing hand. He opened his eyes and saw, as through a cloaking fog, a figure standing above him.

"Who are you?" Yuri asked, his voice small, his Russian now that of his childhood.

"A friend," the figure replied, responding in kind.

Yuri sensed a slight movement by the dream figure and felt a sting in his right arm. "What...is this?" Yuri asked.

"Something to help you rest," the kind voice whispered.

Yuri closed his eyes and felt the warm hand on his forehead once again. He smiled and sighed in contentment.

The hand smoothed a lock of hair from Yuri's forehead and pet him as if he were a child. "Rest, my friend," the voice crooned. "Rest. Rest and dream of pleasant things."

As the hand continued to stroke him, he heard the humming of an old Russian lullaby. The heart monitor nearby slowed down as if keeping time, and Yuri's breathing slowly started to subside. He took a deep, contented breath, released it in one long, relaxing exhalation, and floated away.

It is so peaceful here. So very calm and pleasant. Yuri Kutasov smelled supper and he heard his mother call him from the kitchen door. *Yuri! Yuri! It's time to come home, son. It's time!*

Yuri smiled and began to run. *Coming, mother!*

DOS

Sam Spears opened his eyes, instantly awake with total awareness at the very moment the sky began to lighten and the creatures of the night gave over to the inhabitants of the day. Sam had no idea that this was an uncommon attribute.

That the great bulk of humanity made a gradual slide into a state of consciousness was something Sam had never considered. But it was a feature of his makeup that had always served him well, even when not called upon for immediate survival.

Lying very still, without moving his head or giving any other indication that he was awake, he scanned the room. The electric fan paddled lazily overhead in the center of the high ceiling, stirring the heavy tropical air in a languid eddy that caressed as much as it cooled. He cast a sidelong gaze to the woman purring her early-morning dreams at his side. A glossy raven's wing of hair cascaded over her face and round shoulder. The long, smooth flank pinched to a narrow waist that accentuated the voluptuous and sudden swell of hips before sliding into a pair of legs that always caused heads to turn.

Sam reached down and pulled the love-tangled sheets from the foot of the bed and up over her shoulder. As he tucked the sheet gently around her neck, she murmured softly in her sleep, pulled her legs up into herself, and let out a long sigh of contentment.

Sam eased himself from the bed and then stood still a few seconds, listening as the day began to come alive outside. The trade winds of the dry season called through the mostly leafless trees as they picked up speed en route to their eventual daytime velocity of twenty knots. The sounds of the awakening city down below mounted the slopes of Ancon Hill, reaching his house and into his bedroom.

Satisfied that all was normal, Sam picked up the black silk eye patch that rested in a carved wooden bowl on the nightstand, next to his Czech .32, his GI wristwatch, and a metal flashlight. As Sam fitted the cup of the patch over the empty space his left eye had once occupied, he heard a stirring from the bed and the woman turned over. From the change in the sound of her breathing and the altered atmosphere in the room, he knew she was awake.

"Sammy, mi amor?" she purred, her voice still laden with sleep.

"Yes, Blanqui?"

"Why are the...cicatriz? Oh, I don't know the English word."

Sam finished adjusting the eye patch and as he turned to face her, he unconsciously ran his hand down the back of his right thigh.

"The word is 'scar,' my love. Cicatriz, in English, is 'scar,'" he replied.

"Yes, scar," she said, running her eyes over his body. "Why are the scars bigger atras than al frente?

"Those are the exit wounds, mi querida. They're always larger than where the bullets go in," he said as he lightly ran a hand over the four puckered craters that stitched his thigh from knee to groin.

"Do they give you much pain?" she breathed as she openly admired, as she always did, the lean, hard lines of his thighs. Cicatriz and all.

Sam considered a second before answering. "No, not much. Well, sometimes—when it rains."

"Oh pobrecito," she cooed, "but it always rains in Panamá."

Sam's mouth twitched. "So it does, but not so much right now, during the dry season."

Blanquita Villanueva threw off the sheet and stretched her long legs. She reached her arms out to Sam and lifted a knee so as to open her thighs in invitation.

"Come back to bed, Sam. Love me again," she pouted, her full lips curving in a smile.

Sam's body betrayed his desire for the beautiful woman on his bed. He came over to the bed slowly and stood close to her.

"Do we have time? Doesn't your husband return today?" he asked, teasingly.

Blanquita leaned forward and took Sam in her hand. She gave him a smile and a caress.

"Not until this evening. The flight from Mexico," she said.

"Who could resist? But I do have work to do, later today," he replied as she pulled him to her.

"But not until you finish your work here," she murmured as their bodies merged.

* * * *

Sam descended from Quarry Heights in the Canal Zone and crossed into Panamá City proper. At ten in the morning the streets were thronged with pedestrians, buses, and autos. Car horns sounded in what was known as the Panasecond, that brief instant in time between the car in front not moving fast enough and the driver behind hitting his horn.

Sam was in no hurry. He continued downhill through the party and club district centered on Calle J, past the famed and infamous Ancon Inn, threading his way through the rat's warren of streets leading eventually to the waterfront. Then traffic came to a jolting halt at the intersection with Avenida Central. Oddly, no horns were blaring, thanks, no doubt, to the Guardia Nacional corporal standing at the intersection.

Sam leaned out the window of his car and called respectfully, "Oye, Sargento. Qué pasa con el trafico? Hay choque alla?"

The corporal did not mind being called sergeant so he didn't correct Sam. Sam's long-established tactic of addressing any military member with at least one rank higher than his insignia displayed was a small act of courtesy, as he saw it, which had never failed to pay dividends.

The corporal turned and the first thing he noted was the sticker on the windshield of Sam's car showing registration in the Canal Zone. He stepped over and leaned to get a better look inside. It wasn't unheard of, but it wasn't often, that he met a gringo who spoke Spanish—particularly with a Panamanian accent—and this in itself put Corporal Menendez in a more receptive frame of mind than was his usual.

"No wreck, señor. A demonstration. The university students are making protest," he replied in the Spanish dialect of the Panamanian interior.

Sam smiled at the mahogany-hued corporal, dressed in his gleaming spit-shined boots, sharply pressed starched fatigues, and squared cap. The members of La Guardia Nacional always looked parade ready.

"Better than sitting in class all day. And much more exciting," Sam remarked with a grin. "But it does make *your* job more difficult."

Corporal Menendez squared his shoulders and thought, *This is a man who understands matters.* "We serve the public interest, señor."

"And in excellent fashion too, I must say," Sam returned. "But La Guardia has no orders to break up the demonstration?"

"We are instructed to watch and keep matters calm. The students cause no problems, we give them no problems."

"A wise policy, Sargento."

Sam looked around at the stalled traffic on each side and asked, "Do you think Avenida Ancon is open down to Casco Viejo?"

Corporal Menendez lifted the shiny brass whistle that hung from a loop of chain attached to the button of his left breast pocket. He gave a sharp blast and motioned to the car directly behind Sam to back up.

"Sí, señor. Go back two blocks and turn onto Avenida Ancon. From there you will have no problem getting to the Old City."

Sam touched his forehead in a two-finger salute. "Gracias, Sargento. Que le pasa un buen dia."

"Igualmente, caballero," the corporal replied.

Sam pulled out and maneuvered back through the stalled traffic while Corporal Menendez turned to watch the leading edge of the demonstration as it approached his position.

Rabi blancos! Pampered rich kids! thought Menendez as the university students passed by shouting their slogans and waving hand-lettered banners. His sentiment would be echoed by almost everyone who was stuck in the rapidly building snarl of traffic that would take Menendez and his La Guardia comrades many thankless hours to untangle.

TRES

Sam swiveled in his wooden office chair, unthinkingly touched his eye patch, and spoke into the old-fashioned desk phone, a relic from the thirties.

"Tell the governor there's no threat to the canal. I was just down there and it's all as orderly as a Methodist church picnic."

Sam listened a bit and then responded, "No! Absolutely not. There is no reason to call out the Canal Zone Police. If he did that it would be like a red flag waved in front of a bull. The students are protesting Arosemena's budget cuts to the university, not gringo depredations in Panamá. Play it calm and keep a low profile. For a change, this isn't our problem."

Sam listened again before replying, "I have some boys keeping an eye on it, and if anything changes I'll let you know."

Another pause, eyes to the ceiling. "Okay, Trotter, I will. My best to the missus, and I'll see you both at the reception. Luego."

He turned to see his secretary, Marta Fonseca, standing patiently in the doorway, a single sheet of paper in her hand. Marta had been with him, what? Six? Seven years now? Since he opened the office back in '45. She hadn't been a debutante even then, but it seemed to Sam that she had hardly aged in the intervening years. She wasn't what you'd call a beautiful woman—handsome came to mind—but she had an indefinable, highly attractive quality that always made men stop and admire her. There was also a strength to her that caused most men to tread carefully in her presence. Sam hung up the phone and saw the serious look on her face.

"Dime, Marta. What is it?"

Marta crossed to Sam's desk and handed him the folded sheet of paper.

"Just in from Contadora, Samuel. Eyes Only, for you," she said in a rich alto voice.

Sam took the sheet, slit it open, and gave it a quick read. "Gracias, Marta. Will you close the door and give me a few minutes?"

She was already pointed that way. "Hold your calls too?" she asked as she headed out.

"You anticipate me, mi amor." He nodded thanks, watching her smile at him over her shoulder before she closed and locked the door, leaving him alone.

Sam spun his chair around to face a tall RCA Victor combination phonograph and radio set. He turned on the radio, tuning to the American Forces Network station at Fort Clayton in the

Canal Zone, and turned up the volume to Slim Whitman's *Indian Love Call.* He had no interest in the music. He took a key that hung on a string around his neck and opened a bottom set of doors in the cabinet, revealing a small built-in steel safe.

Three turns on the safe's dial and it opened. Sam pulled out what seemed to be, but wasn't, a thick notepad. Back at his desk, he confirmed the date on the calendar—21 January 1952—and opened a one-time pad codebook to the appropriate page. Pencil in hand, scanning back and forth between the Eyes Only message and the one-time codebook, he quickly deciphered the message:

INMATE FATALITY.

...WALTER DRISCOLL

"Damn it all!" Sam swore. "Not again."

He took up a blank sheet of paper and, using the one-time codebook again, wrote a new message. He double-checked what he had written in code and then tore the used sheet from the codebook before locking it back in the safe. Then he lit both the original message and the codebook page with a battered Ronson lighter and held them until they were well aflame before dropping both into the metal wastebasket. He watched until they were totally consumed and then stirred the ashes to a dusty powder.

"Marta!" he called.

The door opened instantly and Marta was there, poised with pen and pad, ready for instructions he delivered in rapid-fire sequence.

"Call Chaplain O'Neil, please—he's at the Fort Amador Chapel today. Tell him to change into civvies and that Cholo will pick him up at his office in thirty minutes. He needs to pack an overnight bag and bring what he needs to conduct a funeral service. Have Cholo take the Willys and bring Father Mike to Albrook Airfield. Call Lieutenant Gaddis and tell him I need the plane ready in half an hour. I'll give him the destination when I get there. Can do?"

"Por supuesto," she answered, not bothering to look up from her notebook.

He handed her the message he had written. "And then telex this to Washington. Eyes Only for Broadstreet."

Marta took the message and spun on her heels, saying, "'I'm on it, Samuel," as she hurried back to her office.

Sam stood. From the center desk drawer he took out a compact Czechoslovak .32-caliber automatic. He pushed the slide back a fraction of an inch and checked the chamber to make sure he had one up the spout before clicking the safety back into position and tucking the pistol into the offside waistband of his trousers. From the hat rack in the corner he took a well-tailored safari jacket and Panamá hat and put them on. From the closet he retrieved a battered AWOL bag and last, he snagged a gnarled and knotted walking stick resting against the doorframe.

Ready for action, Sam strode from the room. Only someone who knew him well would have been able to detect the slight limp that caused him to favor his right leg.

* * * *

Private Jimmy Burns stepped from the guard shack and admired the cream-colored 1950 Ford Coupe as it turned from Gaillard Highway and into the entrance to Albrook Army Airfield. It was the very model Jimmy lusted for, but it was out of the question on his private's monthly salary of eighty-five dollars and eighty cents—before taxes and contributions to the unit fund. Maybe when he got back home to Alabama and was earning real money in his dad's roofing business. But for now, it was buses and the shoe-leather express for Private Burns.

As the car neared, Jimmy stepped from the shade of the shack's overhanging roof and held up his hand in a signal for the car to halt. At that instant, there was a light tap on his shoulder and he felt a heavy shadow fall over him as Sergeant Turner stepped to his side.

"I'll take this one, Burns," the sergeant announced in a deep-throated rumble.

The car came to a halt in front of the sergeant's outstretched hand. Master Sergeant Nolan Turner, all six foot three inches and two hundred-plus trim pounds of him, carefully looked the car over before stepping to the driver's window and leaning in.

"Major, your base sticker expires at the end of the month. What say I get you a new one and bring it to your office?" Turner said with a sudden grin.

Sam stuck his hand out the window in greeting. Turner grabbed it and gave it a friendly pump.

"Nolan Turner, you old reprobate! What are you doing on gate duty? You piss off the general again?" Sam asked.

Turner jerked a thumb over his shoulder. "Breaking in a new man. I like to do these things myself. Let 'em know what I expect. Keeps 'em outta trouble in the long run."

"Still the same old mother hen, I see."

"Maybe, but not much longer, sir. I retire the end of next month."

"Twenty years already?"

Turner nodded. "Twenty-two. Hard to believe it myself."

"What are your plans then? What does Dolores have to say about retirement?"

Turner rubbed the back of his neck and squinted his eyes in thought. "She loves it here, you know. So do I. All her family's here, and me, I got none left in the States. Been here since the war, but the Canal Zone's not hiring new police officers just now, and there's little other calling for an old infantry sergeant. But I guess we can get by 'til something shows itself."

Sam thought a second, then said, "What say you come work for me, Nolan? I'll pay you three times what the army does, and we can get you and Dolores a nice Canal Zone house in Balboa."

Turner's face split into a huge grin. "That would be great, sir, but as a what? What would I be doing?"

"You'd be my Top Kick, my Field First. Just like the old days. Only better. With neither of us having to put up with geriatric generals and calcified colonels."

Turner let out a whoop of laughter. "Ah, Major, you always had the turn of a phrase right on the tip of your tongue. Yes, sir! I accept. I couldn't think of anything better than that. And Dolores will be tickled to no end."

Sam put the car in gear. "Good! When you bring the sticker over we'll get your paperwork started. You know where my office is, in Casco Viejo, the Old City?"

"I do," Turner replied with a brisk nod.

"All right then! Good to have you back, Top."

Sergeant Turner stood to attention and gave Sam a crisp salute. "Good to be with you again, Major."

Sam returned the salute as Turner motioned him through the gate. When Sam had gone, Private Burns looked closely at his sergeant before hesitantly asking, "Sarge, you saluted that civilian, and even called him 'Major.' Who is he?"

Turner watched Sam's car drive away and then turned his attention to Private Burns. "Major Spears was my commander in Burma during the war. He was the best officer and the finest soldier I ever knew." He plucked a stray thread dangling from the seam of Burns' khaki shirt and pointed with his chin toward an oncoming vehicle. "Back to work, Jimmy. You handle 'em now. Try not to mess it up. And as far as salutes go—when in doubt, whip one out."

* * * *

Sam parked at the edge of the apron between a 1949 Willys wagon and a new racing-green MG Midget. Standing ready on the apron was a four-seat single-engine plane, with three men standing nearby. He got out, AWOL bag in one hand, walking stick in the other, and headed over to join the group.

He shook hands with the army chaplain, Father Mike O'Neil, and the young pilot, Lieutenant Eddy Gaddis. He gave a nod to Cholo Martinez, his all-around Man Friday: a square-shouldered man with a dark, rugged face and steady eyes that looked out at the world from under constantly lowered brows.

"Father, Lieutenant—thanks for responding on such short notice. We've something urgent to attend to on Contadora. Are we ready to fly?"

"I've checked with flight ops, Major. There's no traffic in the area. We can depart anytime you like," Gaddis said.

"My things are aboard," offered Father O'Neil.

"Then let's saddle up," Sam ordered.

Lieutenant Gaddis reached for Sam's bag. "Give me your bag, sir. I'll stow it aboard and then we can kick the tires and light the fires."

"Thanks," said Sam. "Give me a minute and I'll be right with you."

While the chaplain and Gaddis headed to the plane, Sam turned to Cholo and said, "Cambiame las llaves."

The men exchanged car keys, with Sam taking the keys to the Willys and Cholo those of the Ford. As they did, Sam gave Cholo instructions. "Take my car back to the office. Stay at my place tonight. There's food and beer in the refrigerator. I should be back by tomorrow, if everything goes well. If not, I'll send a message to Marta. Until then, make it look like I'm still in town. Entiendes?

"Claro, jefe," Cholo returned.

"Bueno. Estas armado?" Sam asked.

Martinez opened the left side of his jacket just enough to give Sam a glimpse of the big .45 automatic pistol nestled in the shoulder holster beneath his armpit.

"Como siempre," he said, speaking in his habitual quiet voice. Cholo wasn't about noise.

Sam clapped him on the shoulder and hurried to the plane. The engine came to life as soon as Sam was buckled in, and within minutes Lieutenant Gaddis had the plane gathering speed down the runway, gaining lift, and taking off in the direction of the Pacific mouth of the Panamá Canal.

Sam watched carefully as the plane gained altitude. To the left was Ancon Hill and Quarry Heights and just beyond, the city of Panamá. The Canal Zone town of Balboa with its wharves and dry dock was directly below them. Just over the mouth of the canal, Gaddis turned the plane onto its flight heading. The canal's waters were filled with traffic. Some ships were anchored and awaiting transit through the canal; others were headed either in toward the locks and the Atlantic or out into the open Pacific.

On the right bank was a place that always intrigued Sam, though he had never visited and probably never would: the Palo Seco leper's colony was nestled off by itself in a clearing in the jungle. Then the mainland was behind them. Ahead were the islands of Toboga and Taboguilla and after that, just a narrow smudge on the horizon more than twenty miles away was the Perlas Archipelago and Isla Contadora.

* * * *

As they drew near the island of Contadora, Lieutenant Gaddis began a wide descending turn for final approach. Then he chopped power and the plane settled to a landing so gentle it was almost unnoticeable. They taxied to an apron where a jeep and several men stood waiting.

When Gaddis killed the engine, Sam climbed down to the tarmac, grabbed his walking stick, and gave Father Mike a hand getting out of the back seat. Then he turned to meet Agent Walter Driscoll as he ambled over to greet the arriving party.

"I didn't think you'd be here so soon, Sam," Driscoll said as he gave Sam a handshake of greeting.

"Walt, you know Father O'Neil and Lieutenant Eddy Gaddis, don't you?"

"Sure," Driscoll replied. "How are you, Father, Lieutenant?"

As Driscoll greeted the other men, Sam ran his eyes over the man. Walter Driscoll, he recalled, had been a top investigator in the FBI and had been recruited into the CIA for his skills as an interrogator. For the past year he had been the head of background investigation and verification here on Contadora. Sam knew him as a skilled professional but lately, things had been going awry here. Sam thought he knew where the problem lay. He didn't know how much of the blame belonged at Driscoll's doorstep, but he was determined to find out.

"Walt, Father Mike, Eddy, and I will need quarters for the night," Sam said.

Driscoll turned to two uniformed armed guards standing near the jeep. "Chambers, Moffitt! Put these men's bags in the jeep and then you can return to your duties."

Sam knew Chambers by sight. He was a ruddy-faced, powerfully built former Marine. He gave Driscoll a quick nod and led his partner to the plane to heft the baggage.

Sam studied Moffitt out of the tail of his eye, thinking. The man was medium height with an almost delicate-looking build. His dark wavy hair stood in stark contrast to his fair complexion. He was somewhere in his mid-twenties and looked like a desk jockey that had never spent a day outdoors in his life.

Moffitt, you're out of place here, Sam thought. *You look more like an office clerk than a soldier. So, what, my lad, are you doing on this island where everything bites?*

Sam watched thoughtfully as the two guards pitched the bags into the jeep and the guests clambered aboard. Driscoll took the wheel and cranked up. As they pulled away, Sam exchanged a glance with Chambers.

Chambers met Sam's eyes steadily, then turned away to continue his rounds. As Sam looked back over his shoulder, Moffitt was walking slowly and wincing as though his jungle boots hurt his feet.

CUATRO

The air in the room was so cold Sam could almost see his breath. All tile and stainless steel, it looked as inhuman as it felt. Sam studied the dead body lying on the gurney and thought a few more seconds before looking up at the man standing on the other side of it.

"Doctor Gottlieb, can you tell me what happened?" Sam's voice was as chilly as the air in the room.

Dr. Sidney Gottlieb, late thirties, gave Sam a look of pure contempt. Sam had seen this look many times. It was as much a part of the doctor's persona as his Central European accent and clubbed foot. Gottlieb viewed all other men as intellectual inferiors. Sam thought the physical impediment was the likely cause of Gottlieb's disdainful attitude—a compensation of some sort. But at the end of the day, Sam didn't really care what made the man such an overbearing ass. He was, Sam thought, the very caricature of the Nazi doctors and scientists the U.S. had brought over after the war.

"A delayed adverse reaction to the interrogation chemicals. The ultimate cause of death was respiratory failure," Gottlieb pronounced.

Sam looked down on the body and reverently pulled the sheet up over the man's wax-hued face. He then looked at Driscoll standing quietly at the foot of the gurney before slowly turning his full attention back to Gottlieb.

"Doctor, if I may. The purpose of this project is to determine the bona fides of these men. These agents. To find out whether they are genuine walk-ins or if they are Soviet plants and double agents. Our purpose here is most assuredly *not to kill them.*"

"Sam," Driscoll interjected. "This was an unforeseeable accident. A stroke of bad luck."

"Walter, this was the *third* unforeseeable accident—the *third* stroke of bad luck in the last four months. It is inexcusable."

Gottlieb flared with heat and condescension. "We can expect a few setbacks. The combination of these chemicals has never been used in this fashion before. It is to be expected—the normal course of events to be expected in experimental medicine."

Sam reached up and touched the band at the corner of his eye patch before responding. Marta would know the gesture. It was an unconscious tic that indicated he was working to contain himself.

"*Primem non nocere.* Do you remember that phrase, Doctor, or was it not part of the curriculum at Heidelberg?" Sam queried.

"*Primem...?*" Driscoll started to ask.

Gottlieb waved his hand impatiently. "Yes, yes. Primem non nocere. The Hippocratic oath: *first, do no harm*. Under normal medical situations, Mr. Spears, that is applicable. But I must remind you, this is not a normal situation."

"Granted, Doctor," Sam retorted. "This has become an *abnormal* situation. It has become harmful, not only to these men, but to our very mission here—that of sorting fact from fiction. Let me remind you, sir, we gain no intelligence, we learn nothing at all, from dead men."

Gottlieb replied with vehemence, "We are making great strides! Great advances!"

Sam turned the sheet down from the dead man's face and said quietly, "Seems to me, Doctor, we are making only corpses."

Sam covered the man's face again and looked to Driscoll. "Walter, have the body made ready for burial. We will conduct a service this evening. Father Mike will officiate."

Driscoll nodded, "Sure, Sam."

Gottlieb spat, "A funeral? This is asinine! Preposterous!"

"Preposterous, Doctor? That his remains are treated with dignity? This man, Yuri Kutasov, was a fellow human being, and as such he is worthy of our respect. No matter what the motivation that brought him here, he *risked* everything by coming over to us, and ultimately, it *cost* him everything. He had little respect from us in life, but by God, sir, he will have it in death!"

"But a funeral service? The man was a communist—an atheist!" Gottlieb was so angry, spittle was gathering in the corners of his mouth.

"He was born to a Polish mother and was baptized a Catholic. That is a fact, regardless of the political system he lived under," Sam said.

"As you will. But please do not expect me to participate in such a pitiful farce."

Sam smiled. "Doctor, I never expected otherwise."

Gottlieb turned abruptly and clumped from the room, slamming the door so hard behind him the air in the room shook.

Sam turned to Driscoll. "Walt, can you have the boat ready for a sunset service? And will you come with us?"

"Sure, Sam. The boat will be ready, and I'll be there."

"Thanks. And another matter—have Demitrova meet me at the bohio in fifteen minutes."

Worry darted across Driscoll's plain face. "Sam, I don't know if that's wise. Demitrova has become very difficult lately. Angry. Hostile. Violent even. And he blames you, Sam. He blames you, more than anyone else, for his being here."

"Then perhaps we can make use of that anger. Send him to me, will you, Walt?"

Driscoll shook his head. "Okay, Sam. I just hope you know what you're doing."

Sam paused to study Driscoll before making reply. "Walter, you have a thankless job here. But you're the best interrogator I've ever known, the best in the business. You know intuitively what works and doesn't work with a subject. You get at the truth while others waste time chasing down lies and evasions. And you do it no matter how difficult the case or the people you have to work with."

"It's true none of this has been easy. And working with Gottlieb..."

Sam tapped his stick on the floor in emphasis. "Gottlieb has his job to do, but ultimately you are the one charged with sifting fact from fiction and reality from fantasy."

Driscoll's features relaxed. "Thanks for the vote of confidence. It means a lot. And yes, I'll send Demitrova to see you. But don't expect too much from him."

The two men left the room, leaving the body of Yuri Kutasov cold and alone. But not quite as friendless as before.

* * * *

When Sam stepped into the shade of the bohio, it felt as though the temperature dropped twenty degrees. He selected a wooden deck chair and pulled another one over so that they faced each other on a diagonal. He placed his stick on the ground next to his chair then took his hat off and placed it on the upright of another chair. He fished in his pocket for a comb that he quickly ran through his hair and settled back to wait.

From the bohio he could look northward across the spacious, manicured grounds and out to sea. To the east rose the mountains of the Darién running in a wide arc to the south all the way down to the Colombian border.

It was a roadless, primitive place; thick with jungle-clad mountains, wild rivers, and only the occasional Choco or

Embera Indian village. Other than in the regional town of Yaviza, the Panamanian government made almost no effort to assert itself there. Sam probably knew the area as well as anyone, having spent months there before the war with his father, the Smithsonian's director of tropical research in Panamá. Sam had often thought that if he ever wanted to disappear, he could do it easily into the Darién.

He heard footsteps approaching and looked up as Dimitri Demitrova stepped under the roof of the bohio and stood silently, staring out across the grounds as Sam had done. Both men took in, but ignored, the two armed guards patrolling along the shoreline.

Demitrova spoke at last, eyes watching the waves foam the beach, as if he were talking to himself.

"Beautiful, is it not? It doesn't look like a prison at all. Flowers, palm trees, the Pacific Ocean. It is like a scene from a vacation postcard. And that is what makes it such exquisite torture."

"Hello, Dimitri. How are you?" Sam asked pleasantly. A normal conversation. With armed guards.

"A good question. And how is Dimitri? Does anyone know? Does anyone care?" Demitrova turned from the waves at last and held Sam with his eyes. "And how do you expect me to be, Samuel? Happy? Grateful? What attitude should I adopt with my warden? What is the protocol for a prisoner in a gilded cell?"

Sam took up his stick, put on his hat, stood, and stepped out of the shade. "I always find that a stroll helps clear the mind. Walk with me, Dimitri."

Demitrova hesitated a second, but then hurried to catch up as Sam ambled ahead of him casually swinging his walking stick as though window shopping along Avenida Central.

When Sam felt Demitrova at his side, he asked, "Tell me what bothers you, Dimitri. Tell me what gives you pain."

"This is not what I envisioned when I came over to your side. I did not leave one totalitarian system to be enslaved under another!" Demitrova spat. "You promised me freedom, Samuel!" His voice became softer, sadder. "But instead, I am still a prisoner."

Sam stopped and looked him in the eye. "Then tell me, Dimitri, what did you expect? A new Cadillac? A large bank account? A busty blonde and a palm-shaded bungalow in Miami? Washington must clear your background and determine if you're a genuine walk-in, an agent provocateur, or a double. In our shoes you'd do the same. And you *know* what the Russians would do under the same circumstances."

Demitrova broke eye contact, turned, and walked away, speaking over his shoulder and causing Sam to catch up.

"The Russians will never stop looking—for me or the others. It is religious dogma with them: they will hunt us down and kill us every one. The longer I am kept in this place the more likely that event becomes."

"You're safe here, Dimitri. The guards on Contadora face out, not in. They protect against intrusion." Sam pointed his stick toward the two guards working their way across the grounds.

"Samuel, sometimes you are a naive fool," Demitrova said, shaking his head.

Sam and the former Soviet agent reached the shoreline. They stood and watched the waves breaking on the reef just offshore, while a flock of frigate birds dove frantically on a school of baitfish that had been driven to the surface by unseen predators below. Each man lost, momentarily, in his own thoughts.

When the frenzied attack offshore subsided, Sam spoke again. "You call this a prison, Dimitri, and in that, you are correct. It is. But a prison also keeps the rest of the world at bay. And that's why you're here, to protect you until you've been cleared and we can get you resettled. Trust me, Dimitri, the Russians will never find you here."

Demitrova put his face very near Sam's and said in an urgent whisper, "But what if they have someone here, on the inside, and he's killing already? Have you ever considered that possibility? A third death, Samuel! Do you think it is mere coincidence?"

"What do you mean, Dimitri? You've said either too much or you've said too little. Which is it?" Sam asked.

"I was prisoner of the Wehrmacht for a short time, before escaping, during the war. You are aware of that, is in my dossier. From this experience I know something of being in the hands of Germans. What I mean, Samuel, is that if I am to die here it will be by my own hand and not that of a torturer, a German, a so-called doctor."

Demitrova fixed Sam with a pleading look and then said in a small voice, "Help me, Samuel. I don't want to die here. Don't let these men kill me."

Sam held Demitrova's intense gaze for a moment. Then he glanced over his shoulder at the guards, who had stopped in the shade of a mango tree to smoke a cigarette. It was obvious to both men that the guards, though staying outside of earshot, had kept well within gunshot.

Sam clasped his hands atop his walking stick and stared at the ground, tapping it quietly. He reached up to touch his eye patch. "There's a beautiful moon this evening, Dimitri. Only a few days from being full. I like to walk at moonrise. The air then has an especially calming quality that lends itself to mature reflection and contemplation. Join me then, if you've nothing else better to claim your time."

He smiled, tipped his hat, and strolled back in the direction of the headquarters building. Demitrova watched Sam depart. *So elegant with that cane of his,* he thought. Then he sighed and turned, once again, to stare out at the wind-whipped waves and farther, to the dark mountains beyond.

* * * *

The engine of the workboat tied to the dock rumbled contentedly as Sam, Walter Driscoll, and Father Mike waited on its deck. The men watched solemnly as two guards passed a stretcher bearing the shrouded body of Yuri Kutasov over the gunnels to the two deckhands. Sam and Driscoll stepped forward to help bring the body aboard and place it gently aft of the wheelhouse.

Driscoll spoke to the deckhands. "Step ashore and cast off the lines."

The men looked to the captain for orders, but he gave them a wry grin that said, *Go ahead. Humor the man.*

The men climbed back down to the dock, undid the lines, and pitched them aboard. As Driscoll stowed the lines, Sam tapped the captain, a grizzled old Panamanian seaman, on the shoulder and said, "Estamos listo, capitán."

One of the deckhands shoved the bow of the boat away from the dock. As the captain eased the throttle forward, the boat with its crew of the living and the dead pulled away swiftly into the gathering dusk.

The water was calm inside the protective reef, but as they exited through a gap in the coral, they hit short, choppy waves that slapped the boat at quick intervals, making for a pitching and irritating ride. Sam stood near the captain, one hand on an overhead rail, and let his knees flex with the bash of each new wave. Driscoll and the chaplain sat on a bench, gripping the seat, heads bobbing side to side like the pigeons Sam watched walking across the plaza.

The captain glanced behind the boat at something that had caught his eye. He nudged Sam with an elbow, pointed his chin to the rear, and said with a nasty grin, "Oye, amigo. Mire alla. Atras."

Sam looked in the direction the old man indicated. The light was going quickly now, dusk being a decidedly short event in the tropics, and Sam squinted to make out what he could. At first he saw nothing behind them except the boat's wake and the dark shoreline disappearing in the distance. Then he saw a darting movement in the water that was soon followed by another and then another.

Suddenly, it dawned on Sam what he was seeing in the water. Sharks. Effortlessly keeping pace, cruising in the vessel's wake, and sizable. Three of them. Big bastards the size of torpedoes.

Driscoll noticed Sam staring aft and he, too, looked back and saw the fins weaving less than a boat length behind. He started to nudge the chaplain but Sam shook his head in warning. Father Mike already looked queasy. No need to add fear to his misery yet. Walter nodded his understanding.

Sam asked the captain. "Cómo se saben? How do they know?"

The old captain flashed a toothless grin. "We take the garbage out to sea in this boat. They know the sound of this engine and always follow us when we come out."

Sam made no reply. He just watched quietly and rocked with the rhythm of the waves. When the light at the end of the dock was no more than a faint red ember bobbing and winking on the horizon, Sam touched the captain's shoulder and said, "Far enough."

The captain prudently brought the boat to a speed just above idle that kept them bow-on to the waves. Sam motioned to Driscoll, who stood, and then the two men lifted the stretcher and balanced it across the gunwale.

Sam looked to the chaplain, still seated with a firm grip on the bench, and said, "Father. It's time."

The chaplain got unsteadily to his feet and came to stand near the head of the stretcher. A large wave hit the boat suddenly, pitching Father Mike forward, and Sam quickly reached over and grabbed him by the arm. The chaplain gave him a thankful glance, then opened his service book and began.

"Lord God, by the power of your Word you stilled the chaos of the primeval seas. You made the raging waters of the Flood subside, and calmed the storm on the Sea of Galilee. As we commit the body of our brother to the deep, grant him peace and tranquility until that day when he and all who believe in you will be raised to the glory of new life promised in the waters of baptism. We ask this through Christ our Lord. Amen."

Sam crossed himself as Father Mike made the sign of the cross over the body. The chaplain then nodded to Sam and Driscoll, who lifted the end of the stretcher to shoulder height and let the weighted body slide overboard.

At the sound of the splash, three dark forms sliced through the rolling water in a boiling swirl. Finding their target, they dove headlong after the sinking corpse. Father Mike looked on in horror as the sharks tore into the shrouded form, batting it back and forth like terriers playing with a ball, tearing it to pieces as it sunk slowly and erratically from view.

The chaplain covered his mouth and gagged "Oh God!" before grabbing the gunnels with both hands and leaning overboard, his body heaving with wet, retching noises.

Sam nodded to the bemused captain and said quietly, "Take us back in."

The captain touched the throttle, deftly turned the boat around, and pointed the bow in the direction of the tiny lights ashore. Sam went to stand next to the chaplain and kept a compassionate hand on his shoulder until the good Father was himself once again.

* * * *

Sam sat at a table by himself in a corner of the camp canteen, head down, writing in a small notebook. There were maybe a dozen other men in the room. Some were finishing a meal while others read, played cards, smoked, or sat talking quietly. Behind the bar a radio mumbled just loudly enough to let you know it existed, but nothing more.

Sam looked up for a few seconds, his eyes fixed on nothing, tapping his teeth with the eraser end of his pencil before he went back to writing again. An unopened bottle of vodka sat on the edge of his table.

Walter Driscoll entered the room and looked around until he saw Sam. He snagged a couple of beers from the bar, made his way over, and sat down, pushing one toward Sam.

"Thought you might like a cold one, but I see you're hitting the hard stuff tonight. Can't say I blame you. That was a pretty rough sight out there."

"The vodka?" said Sam with a shrug. "For a friend. Can't get this brand in the city. How's the chaplain? Is he feeling better?"

Driscoll took a swallow of beer and nodded. "It was a shock but he's okay now. He's hearing confessions in the chapel."

"Father Mike is a good man. Did you know he was in the infantry during the war?" Sam asked before taking a pull on his beer.

Driscoll gave him a surprised look. "I had no idea."

"He was a squad leader in the First Infantry Division. Landed in the first wave at Omaha Beach. Won a Distinguished Service Cross and a battlefield commission at the Battle of the Bulge. Fought through the entire war and never received so much as a scratch. People who knew him then said he always led his platoon from the front. Always took the most dangerous positions himself to save his men. But they also said he was a holy terror to the Germans. Then, after the war ended, he came home and attended seminary. He later reentered the army, and there you are. Father Mike O'Neill, decorated war hero and dedicated Man of Peace."

Sam took another sip of beer before continuing. "I sometimes wonder about him, though. Which persona is the real man—the warrior or the savior? Or is he both in equal parts?"

Driscoll lit a cigarette. "I wouldn't know," he said, blowing a plume of smoke.

"Still, it makes you wonder, doesn't it? What facet of a man will come to the fore under the pressure of extreme circumstances? Which part of him will rise up and prevail when faced with the threat of death—or worse?"

Driscoll shook his head. "Beats me. I've never been in combat."

"But Walter, it's your job to know what makes a man tick. It's what you do."

Driscoll took a slug of beer and lit a new cigarette off the old one. He seemed fidgety. Sam let him fidget. He kept watching as Driscoll nearly drained his beer and wiped his lips. Fidgety.

Driscoll pointed to Sam's notebook and moved to change the subject.

"Writing your report about the...the incident?" he asked.

"Organizing my thoughts." Sam looked at Driscoll while he took a sip from his beer, pretended to study the label for a few seconds, and then set the bottle down neatly on the table. He looked Driscoll straight in the eyes.

"I need the audiotapes, Walt, the tapes of the interrogations. I need copies of all of them. I also want copies of the other postmortems. I want all of this by tomorrow morning." Sam was quiet, but there was no mistaking the concrete in his voice.

Driscoll hunched over the table, glanced around the room as if he feared being overheard, and said, "Sam! That's impossible."

"Walter, I'll have them in the morning or you'll be on the plane with me—bag and baggage—when I leave."

"But Gottlieb—"

"Is not the man who runs this undertaking. He has charge of the medical portion of the program and that is all he has. *You* are charged with conducting the interrogations while *I* am tasked with oversight of the program here in Panamá. I intend to make a detailed review of where we are and seek guidance from the powers on the Potomac."

Driscoll placed his hands flat on the table and sat back. "Sam, we are making good progress here. I am convinced of that."

Sam noted the intensity of Driscoll's manner and the adamant tone of his voice. "Then make sure that's in your report and provide the data to back it up. This isn't a witch hunt, Walter, but the very last one of these men has died under our hand. I'm convinced you are making headway, but I think Gottlieb has become obsessed with his own studies and isn't able to see the larger picture."

Driscoll tried to interject. "But Sam—"

Sam stopped him with a raised hand. "These men are too valuable to be treated like roaches, like laboratory rats. Think of it, Walter! Think what we have here! Think of their worth! Live Soviet agents are rare and precious commodities. Any single one of these men may carry information that could possibly change the current course of the world. We have no idea what kind of intelligence died with those men. What secrets they took to the grave."

Driscoll studied Sam for a bit, rolling things about in his mind. Finally, he stood, a resigned expression on his face.

"I'll have the tapes ready for you in the morning. And the postmortems, along with my report too," he said.

Sam spoke to Driscoll's back as the man left. "Thanks, Walter. Rest well."

Driscoll stopped and looked over his shoulder at Sam. He started to speak, then looked down before finally saying, "Good night, Sam. You too."

Sam watched Driscoll until he had left the room. When he was gone, Sam opened his notebook and wrote a few more lines. Reading it over, and satisfied with the contents, he tore the page from the notebook and then put each in a separate pocket. Sam picked up his hat and cane, tucked the vodka bottle under an arm, and walked from the room.

* * * *

Sam stood at the end of the dock, calmly smoking a cigar and watching as the moon rose fully above the horizon. Footsteps echoing on the wooden planks of the dock alerted him to the approach of another person.

Demitrova stepped to Sam's side, stood silently, and lit a cigarette. Sam waited until his companion had taken a deep draw and then handed him the opened bottle of vodka he carried in his left hand. Wordlessly Demitrova took the bottle, examined the label in the clear moonlight, and took a long, satisfied swallow.

"Ahhh," he sighed, passing the bottle over to Sam. "They don't allow us such luxuries. Beer only for the condemned."

Sam took a sip. At that exact moment, a meteor plunged across the sky in a fiery arc. Sam pointed the bottle toward the path of the space visitor.

"It's customary to make a wish on a falling star," he said as he passed the bottle again.

Demitrova took another long, grateful drink. He dangled the bottle loosely by its neck, lost in contemplation, looking out across the water. Sam waited in patient silence. The only sounds: the steady lap of waves against the shore, the persistent trade winds rustling the palms.

"Wishes," Demitrova breathed. Another pull on his cigarette. "I wish Stalin had never lived. I wish there had never been a war. I wish my mother and father were alive. I wish we still lived together on our little farm in the mountains. I wish I were not here on this island."

He turned to Sam and passed him the bottle.

"That's five wishes, Dimitri. Custom allows only one," Sam corrected.

"Wishes cost nothing, Samuel. They are one of the few genuinely free things in life. I can have as many wishes as I like."

Sam took a sip from the vodka then pointed with it to the boat tied to the dock before passing it back again.

"When the boat's not in use, they take a part from the engine and lock it away in the duty officer's safe. It can't be cranked without the missing part. It's of no use for an escape," Sam pointed out.

"One could always swim," Demitrova replied after a few seconds of thought.

Sam puffed on his cigar and flicked off the clinging ash. "It's no cliché, Dimitri. The greatest concentration of sharks in the world surrounds these islands. They would get any man who tried to swim outside the reef. He wouldn't last more than a few minutes."

"I did not say one would survive. But it is an option. Stay and be killed or take one's chances out there." Again the bottle pointed to the reef and traveled between the men.

Sam turned to face Demitrova. "I need a little time, Dimitri. A little time to make this process function as it should. To make it work to *everyone's* satisfaction."

"I don't believe I have much time, Samuel. I have resisted, but will soon be subjected to chemical interrogation again. I think I am going to die on this island, regardless of your intentions."

Sam put a hand on Demitrova's arm. "Trust me."

Demitrova flipped his cigarette out over the water, the glowing tip scribing a falling star of its own as it fell to the water and disappeared with a hiss.

"As long as I can, Samuel. But I tell you, something is very wrong here. And the right to take a final swim is always mine."

"Don't be in a hurry to make a decision that can't be undone, Dimitri. Besides, there's a lunar eclipse soon—a full one. You wouldn't want to miss that. It's an event that comes only once in a lifetime."

"Once in a lifetime—in a lifetime, once," Demitrova whispered.

Sam reached into his pocket, took out the cap, and screwed it back onto the bottle before handing it over to Demitrova.

"Here, for you. Keep it. I've always hated this stuff."

Demitrova chuckled softly. He hefted the bottle in his hand, and then, with no further word, turned and walked away. Sam stood alone at the end of the dock, finishing his cigar and enjoying the huge tropical moon.

* * * *

Demitrova stood in the open door of his room, also watching the moon, and taking note of the path walked by the two night guards as they made their way across the grounds. On a sudden urge, he turned back into his room and retrieved the bottle of vodka from the nightstand. As he opened it, he fumbled the cap and sent it rolling across the floor. Stooping to pick it up, he noticed something inside. He quickly closed the door and pulled the blinds.

Demitrova sat on the edge of the bed and used a fingernail to pry out a tightly folded piece of paper. He put the cap to one side, unfolded the paper and smoothed it between his fingers, then slowly read the inscription. He looked up with a thousand-yard stare on his face. He read the slip again, his lips moving as he did so.

Rolling the slip of paper into a loose ball, he placed it in his mouth and began to chew. When the paper had been reduced to a slushy mass, he took a slug of vodka from Sam's gift and swallowed. He re-capped the bottle securely and put it on his nightstand and turned out the light.

* * * *

The plane was ready; the engine idling. Lieutenant Gaddis and Father O'Neill were already aboard. Sam and Driscoll stood at the edge of the apron by the jeep as two guards hovered in the near background. Driscoll handed Sam a valise.

"Here you are, Sam. The tapes, the postmortems, and a copy of *my* report."

Sam accepted the bag and replied, "Thanks, Walter. I'll review these before I make my final report. But until further notice, the chemical interrogations are halted."

"Damn it, Sam! We were making such headway. You wouldn't stop us just for an accident!"

"I just did, Walter. Until headquarters makes a ruling, Gottlieb's part of this operation is suspended."

"And if he refuses?" Driscoll asked, real heat in his voice.

“In that case, I will close down this facility,” Sam said in all seriousness.

“Sam, you can’t do that!” Driscoll fired back.

“Oh, but I can. I’m the landlord here, Walter. I contract and pay for the fuel that runs the generators that provides the electricity to power this place. Same thing goes for the food and drink consumed here. For the plane that flies you all in and out and the boats making the deliveries. And everything else that is required to make life possible on what is essentially a desert island. So yes, Walter, I can. I do have that power.”

Driscoll shook his head, scowled, and then looked off into space, grumbling to himself. Sam let him scowl and grumble as long as he wanted. At last Driscoll focused his attention back on Sam.

“I don’t like it, Sam. Not one damn bit,” he said.

Sam spoke quietly, aware the guards were straining to take in what was transpiring between him and their boss. “A good soldier follows orders, even when he doesn’t like them or agree with them. The man who has his ass in a crack from this decision is me. Only me. If Washington doesn’t agree with what I’ve done, you’ll be the second one to know—I’ll be the first.”

A wry smile touched Driscoll’s lips. “Oh hell. I guess you’re right, Sam. Do you want me to handle Gottlieb or do you—”

“I’ve spoken with the good doctor already.”

“How did he take it?”

“As one might expect. Achilles sulks in his tent.”

Driscoll laughed aloud. “At least he’s in character.”

Sam smiled and reached out to shake Driscoll's hand. "You're a good soldier, Walter. Goodbye."

"See you, Sam," Driscoll said as they parted.

Sam turned to go, but then stopped and looked back again. "In case I wasn't clear, Walter. Your interrogations continue, just as you've always done. It's only the chemical interrogations that are suspended until we get a ruling from headquarters."

"Understood, Sam," Driscoll replied. "Safe flight."

"Thanks, Walter—for everything."

Sam took off his Panamá hat and climbed aboard the plane. As they began to taxi into position for takeoff, he spotted Demitrova standing alone off to the side of the runway. The men made and held eye contact. As the wheels of the plane lifted from the ground, Sam raised a hand in a simple gesture of goodbye. Demitrova stared back at him but made no sign of acknowledgment. Then the plane turned to the north, out over the Bay of Panamá, and toward the mainland beyond.

Dimitri Demitrova watched until the plane was a tiny speck in the sky. Then he turned, head down and hands in his pockets, and walked away.

CINCO

"Here, give me those," Marta said as she took Sam's hat, walking stick, and bag.

Sam gave her a peck on the cheek and asked with a flippant grin, "Anything noteworthy happen while I was gone? War? Famine? Earthquakes? A riot or two?"

Marta rolled her eyes toward Sam's inner office. "Mr. Broadstreet arrived this morning. He is waiting in your office."

"Well, that is good news," he said, as he smoothed back his hair, touched his eye patch, and walked in to greet his boss.

Carleton Broadstreet was in his mid-fifties and of medium everything: height, build, and weight. He had the tweedy look of a liberal arts professor at a small New England college—or even an Anglican vicar. His white hair was surprisingly thick for his age and was matched in color by shaggy eyebrows and a full but neatly trimmed mustache. When Sam stepped into the room,

Broadstreet put down the newspaper he was reading and rose to greet his protégé.

Sam took Broadstreet's outstretched hand, put his left arm around the older man's shoulder, and greeted him with a warm abrazo. He stepped back to hold and assess his old friend at arm's length.

"Carleton! My God, that was fast. In fact, I didn't expect you to come down at all, but I am delighted that you did!"

"As I am to be here, my boy," Broadstreet replied. "But what do you mean, fast? I was on a swing through the region and wanted to stop in. I have some news for you. Some things I wanted to speak with you about in person."

"Then you didn't get my message yesterday?"

Broadstreet raised an eyebrow in surprise. "Message? No. As I said, I've been traveling. I arrived here only last night, on the flight from Mexico City."

"Ah well. Then we can bring each other up to speed on events. Have you had breakfast?" Sam asked.

"Nothing yet. I came straight over."

Sam knew Carleton liked his meals. "Then let's take a walk. There's a place nearby that I think you'll like. Jasmine's."

"By all means, Samuel, lead the way," Broadstreet said, patting his stomach.

Marta handed Sam his barely settled hat and cane as the two men passed through the outer office.

"Estarémos al restaurante Jasmina, mi amor. Y por favor, dile a Cholo a seguirnos con el Ford," Sam said as he squared the brim of his hat over his brow. The precaution of having Cholo follow the men with the Ford seemed prudent for several reasons.

"Of course, Samuel," she said, beginning to dial as the men went out the door.

Sam and Carleton Broadstreet strolled in companionable silence down the narrow cobblestone streets of Panamá's Old City—the colonial district known as Casco Viejo. The multistoried buildings shaded the narrow lanes and made for a surprisingly cool atmosphere. Sam loved this area of the city. With its balconies, ornamental ironwork, and window boxes spilling over with vibrantly colored tropical flowers, the Old City looked more French than Spanish.

There were surprisingly few people on the streets. One old woman was slowly sweeping the sidewalk across the way. At the end of the block approaching them was a painfully thin, ancient-looking man pushing a rickety vegetable cart via one badly twisted leg. On the front of the cart, a rusty cowbell clapped and sang as the cart's wheels jolted over the cobbles.

Sam stopped briefly and spoke to the vendor.

"Unos mangos y una bolsa de naranjas, Don Julio." Sam put two dollars into the man's hand. "Dejalos a la oficina con doña Marta." The mangos and oranges would be chosen with care and delivered personally to Marta.

The old man gave Sam a wet and toothless smile. "Gracias, joven," he replied as he tucked the bills into his shirt. "Que le pasa un buen dia."

"Igualmente, abuelo." Sam gave the old grandfather a respectful touch to the brim of his hat.

As the two men continued on their way and the vendor was out of earshot, Broadstreet said to Sam, "I understand enough Spanish to know you could have made that purchase for fifty cents or less."

Sam explained to his friend as they walked on. "In this district alone there are six foreign embassies, four Panamanian ministry buildings, and the presidential palace. Not to mention the homes of any number of wealthy and influential people. Don Julio is a fixture here—he visits them all. And to the ricos, he is little more noted than a stray cat. In essence, he is invisible. But he sees and hears things that would utterly amaze you. When he drops the fruit off with Marta in a few minutes, she will sit him in a comfortable chair and give him a glass of rum and one of my cigars.

"There, he will sip and smoke and tell her all the notable things he's seen, and all the neighborhood gossip that he's heard from the area's maids, cooks, chauffeurs, and yard boys in the last week. Marta will take it down in shorthand and I'll have a transcript on my desk no later than this afternoon. While he's there he'll also pick up his sueldo, that is to say, his salary, for the week. And come Christmas there will be a nice bonus as a present for his wife."

Broadstreet nodded his admiration. "Sounds like a wonderful street agent you have there."

Sam gave him a sideways grin. "He is. And so are the five others we have, in various capacities, around the city. Different, but each one equally as good as Don Julio."

"I've never seen them referenced on your expense account," Broadstreet remarked.

Sam shrugged. "Nor will you. What cost there is I pay from my own pocket. It's mainly a matter of treatment and respect. The haves here treat the have-nots as vermin. I treat them as humans. It's amazing what benefits that will bring to your door."

As the two men approached a corner, Sam noticed a vertical white chalk mark waist high on the cut-stone wall of a building fronting the street. Sam unobtrusively took the stub of a piece of yellow chalk from his pocket and made a quick cross mark over the white slash as he walked by. If Broadstreet noticed, he made no comment. They crossed to the next block and were soon at a small café perched at the very end of Calle 5 overlooking the seawall of the baluarte and out on to the Bay of Panamá.

Sam steered Carleton to a side table next to the seawall rail. As they took seats, a middle-aged lady with a dazzling smile and surprising blue eyes in her brown face took the men's hats and placed them on a chair.

"Buenos dias, Sammy," she said. "Señor," she nodded to Broadstreet. "Quieren los caballeros un café?"

"Muy buenas dias, Doña Jasmina. Café sí. Y dos ordenes, tambien, de mi desayuno usual, por favor," Sam said, indicating he was ordering also for his friend.

"Inmediatamente, caballero," she replied, placing napkins in each man's lap. As she returned to the kitchen with their order, she motioned to a boy waiting by the doorway, who hurried over with coffee.

"Gracias, joven," Sam said as the boy finished filling the cups and retreated to his station, where he could keep a sharp eye on the patio.

The men took an appreciative sip of coffee. Sam turned his chair to an angle so that his good eye was on Broadstreet. He crossed his legs and leaned back comfortably. Broadstreet put his cup down, placed a forearm on the table, and leaned forward to begin the conversation.

"It's your bailiwick, Sam. You go first," Broadstreet said.

"We had another death at the facility on Contadora. I sent you an advisory message yesterday as soon as I was informed, then went out to take the pulse of the operation. I fear that Gottlieb is swimming entirely too far from shore when it comes to his part of the program. He's more concerned, I believe, with conducting experiments than with fulfilling the principal aim of the project."

Broadstreet evinced no surprise. He nodded slightly to acknowledge Sam's report and asked, "First of all, who died?"

"Kutasov," Sam replied. "The NKVD agent who came over to us in Italy."

Broadstreet winced. "We expected much from him. He had spent time in the Kremlin, in the Supreme Soviet. He was a potential mother lode of information."

Sam nodded his agreement. "But no more."

"His loss is a hard pill to swallow. What action have you taken, Sam?"

"I've halted the chemically enhanced interrogations until we can make a thorough review of the program and decide how to proceed. The standard interrogations under Walter Driscoll and his team are to continue. On your end, I'd like headquarters to take an independent look at the mixture and dosage of the drugs being used. I have a feeling that's where we'll find the fault of these deaths lies."

"I think that's a prudent decision, Sam. But there may be some objections at headquarters. You know there's a lot of pressure from on high to get results, to find out if these men are attempted doubles or genuine walk-ins. But by couching this as a medical precaution it may give us some traction."

"Thanks, Carleton. I didn't take this step lightly. But we can't afford to keep losing these men. Dirty or not, genuine or plants, these men are too valuable to let slip needlessly through our fingers."

"I couldn't agree more, Sam."

"I'll send you my full report as soon as I've reviewed Driscoll's account and listened to the recordings of the interrogations. It should only be a couple of days. Now then, to what do I owe the pleasure of your most very welcome, if unexpected, visit?

At that moment, Jasmina approached bearing a large wooden tray laden with steaming plates. The aroma wafting from the tray was mouthwatering, and Carleton Broadstreet gave the contents a hungry look as Doña Jasmina deftly placed the meal on the table.

"Disculpe, caballeros," she said as she arranged the meal on the table.

"Gracias, mi amor," Sam replied, smiling his hunger and thanks.

"No hay de qué. Buen provecho, señores," she said with a slight curtsy, and then headed back to her kitchen kingdom.

Sam pointed to the platters with his knife and fork. "As the lady said, 'buen provecho'—dig in."

The men filled their plates and began to eat with attention and appreciation. Once the sharp edge was off their appetites, Sam and Carleton picked up their conversation once again.

"I'm making a swing through Latin America, Sam," the older man said, waving his fork for emphasis, or perhaps to indicate direction. "Checking in with our embassies and residents, seeing firsthand what we lack and where."

"For the purpose of...?" Sam asked as he put two empanadas on Carleton's plate and another on his own.

"Most of the interagency warfare in Washington has finally been settled—and settled in our favor. Nineteen fifty-two is going to be a year of great change for us, my lad. Hoover and the FBI have lost their mandate for intelligence collection in the Americas. It falls now within our charter."

"What about the armed services? Army and naval intel? Where do they shake out in this?" Sam asked. "They've always had their own bailiwicks around the world and have guarded them like jealous mother hens."

"Those were the easy ones, Sam," Broadstreet replied with a smile. "The only thing the director needed to say was 'Pearl Harbor' and that ended the discussion. Truman made the decision on the spot. The services maintain their brief as to Soviet order of battle and weaponry, but they are out of the business of running agents and collecting human intelligence. The old order has been totally revamped. And we, Central Intelligence, are the dominant component of the new structure."

"How so?" Sam asked, a carimañola heading into his mouth.

"The Agency now has an enhanced mandate. Truman has signed off on our new charter. Beginning with this year, we are going to take a decidedly more proactive stance. At the national level that sorts out as follows: Eisenhower will be the new president. Director Beddel Smith, after leading the fight for us in Washington, is retiring and will be replaced by current deputy director for operations, Mr. Allen Dulles. Whose brother, John Foster Dulles, will be the new secretary of state.

"Both those men have great experience in international affairs. Together they wield substantial power in Washington and are in complete agreement that America should henceforth enact a more vigorous and muscular clandestine foreign policy."

Sam stopped eating in surprise. "That's a little fast for me, Carleton. So back up a bit. You say *Eisenhower* will be elected? But it's only January. The conventions aren't until later in the summer. No one—of either party—has even been nominated yet."

"Oh Sam. Sometimes your political naïveté is really touching. It seems I have dreadfully neglected your education in these matters. So let me explain: the power brokers of the nation have made their decision, and they have decided that Eisenhower will be president."

"Power brokers? And who might they be, Carleton? Enlighten me on that little matter, if you will."

"I sometimes forget that you've never really lived in the States and aren't quite aware of the way of things. So in the name of simplicity let me just say: *Wall Street.* The men who make the major decisions of finance, commerce, and law have determined that the end of the Roosevelt era has finally arrived. We are decisively engaged with the Soviet Union for world dominance, and it is a struggle in which we cannot, and must not, fail. General Eisenhower is a man of proven strength. He is a man of decisive leadership and far-reaching vision. He has the confidence of the American people. He is trusted by our allies and respected—even feared—by the Russians. He comprehends what we are up against in this struggle and has the fortitude to do what we must."

Sam gave this some thought before replying. "Okay, Carleton, I'll go along with what you say. Ike will sit in the Oval Office and Dulles will be our new director. But what does that mean specifically for us?" Sam asked.

"It means, my boy, that we shift from the defensive to the offensive. We solidify our positions around the world and simultaneously confront the Soviets on every front, in every corner of the globe. Which brings me to the main purpose of my trip. First of all, I want you to take over operations for all of Latin America—from the Texas border to Tierra del Fuego. No one knows the region as well as you, Sam, or has a greater feel for the sensibilities of the hemisphere."

Sam sipped his coffee and looked at Broadstreet over the rim of his cup, stalling a beat before answering. He put down his cup and shook his head. "It's too large, Carleton. Too large and varied a region for one man to handle alone."

"Oh, you would have subordinates in place," Broadstreet said.

"Yes, but still, there are several subregions that are so distinct, so unique, they should be handled as different entities. May I make a few suggestions?" Sam asked.

"By all means," Broadstreet said with a wave of the hand that meant *go ahead.*

"Let's handle Mexico separately; make her the responsibility of one man. I'd recommend you assign a Mormon who has done his mission service in Mexico. There have been Mormon families down there for more than a hundred years, and they know the country better than any other Americans—and we have some excellent Mormon agents in the service."

"That sounds reasonable. What else?"

"I'll take Central America, the Caribbean, and the northern shoulder of South America: Colombia, Ecuador, Venezuela, and the Guyanas. Those are the countries most susceptible to communist ideology and the region where it has found some fertile ground among the university students and the campesinos."

"Done, Sam. It's yours."

Sam gave Broadstreet a nod and continued. "Handle Brazil as a separate country—they're not there yet, but Brazil is going to develop into a real power in the coming decades. Next, treat Peru, Chile, and Bolivia as a joint region. The same goes for Argentina, Uruguay, and Paraguay. The Russians will never get a foot in those last three countries. They're still not over their infatuation with the Nazis."

Broadstreet had been methodically packing his pipe while Sam talked. He took out his lighter, touched it to the bowl, and puffed. "I see you've given this some thought already."

"Daydreamed, I think, is the better term."

Broadstreet blew a cloud of smoke and smiled. "Rather lucid daydreams, I would say. It will call for some good men."

"I can advise in their selection, if you'd like," Sam said, lifting his coffee cup for another sip.

"I'd like. Now. To the specifics here, as our prefect of Panamá, what will you need?"

Sam thought a second before replying, "Send me a new agent, Carleton, a young man, someone who's not yet been in the field. I don't want him to have to unlearn someone else's methods. Nor do I want a lawyer either, but rather someone with a degree in finance or business. A Spanish speaker would be nice, but that's not a showstopper; he can learn. And while I'm asking, I'd like him to have had military service and have seen action in the combat arms. I don't want a chair-borne ranger or some congressman's son who was a general's aide."

Broadstreet chuckled at that last bit. "Anything else, Sam? You still haven't told me what resources you will need here."

"I want a bank, Carleton. A bank that we and we alone control, to handle clandestine transactions. A setup like the French intel service has in Indochina. I want to be able to move funds as surreptitiously as possible, and Panamá is the perfect location from which to accomplish that. We can use it to service the entirety of Latin America. Also, I intend to form a Panamanian import-export company and use that as my raison d'être. My cover as Canal Zone security coordinator is getting long in the tooth and beginning to wear a little thin."

Broadstreet took another contemplative pull on his pipe. "Yes, I like both those, all of those, ideas. I'll find you a good man. And a bank is no problem. The Agency, as you know, is full of Wall Street bankers. We can place a branch of an American firm here for that purpose. Now, what are we to do with this current Panamanian president? He's becoming more and more unmanageable. The view in Washington is that he's getting almost as difficult as Árbenz in Guatemala."

"I think we can ease him out without too much trouble. He's managed to alienate the students, and more importantly, the business class is becoming increasingly leery of him. I have influential contacts within both the major political parties. And I've a senior La Guardia commander that heads a coterie of like-minded officers who will be only too happy to give a subtle push when the time comes. But I hope to do it as easily as possible. In the aftermath I'd rather our fingerprints not be found at the scene."

"Sound thinking, Samuel. And in normal times I'd leave it all to your discretion. But these are not normal times. It is a political imperative that President Arosemena has to be gone prior to the U.S. general election. So if soft measures prove of no avail, then be very prepared to pursue a harsher course of action."

Sam placed his cup carefully on the table. "I will, Carleton. I just want, if at all possible, to effect the change without bloodshed."

"That's understandable, Samuel. But make sure, blood or no blood, that he is gone well before the first Tuesday in November."

Sam placed a hand lightly over his heart and smiled. "I hear, oh Caesar, and I obey."

Broadstreet chuckled. "Oh Sam. Even when serious, you make jest."

Sam caught sight of Doña Jasmina hovering to the side, coffeepot in hand. He held up a finger and glanced from her to Broadstreet. "Something else? More coffee?" he asked his boss.

"Thank you, no, I've had enough." Broadstreet placed a hand on his midriff and gave it an appreciative pat. "It was a delicious meal. Someday you'll have to tell me what all we ate."

Sam waved Doña Jasmina off with a smile of thanks. The men stood to depart. Sam picked up his cane and handed Broadstreet his fedora. "Where are you staying?" Sam asked as he adjusted the strap of his eye patch and then fitted his own hat at just the right angle.

"I'm the guest of your erstwhile boss and my old friend, the Canal Zone governor, General Newcomer."

Sam put several bills on the table and his coffee cup on top. He pointed to Doña Jasmina and then to the cup. She nodded and smiled that she understood. Sam blew her a kiss.

"Then you'll be at the reception this evening?" Sam asked.

"Of course. And you. Will I see you there?" Broadstreet inquired.

"With bells on. Melba—Mrs. Newcomer—would skin me alive if I failed to appear at one of her soirees. And I understand this is an important one," Sam grinned.

"Good. Now, if you don't mind, I'd like to use your office to catch up on my messages and then perhaps your man can drive me to my quarters?" Broadstreet nodded down the avenue to where Cholo was parked in Sam's Ford Coupe. "I see he just happens to be conveniently nearby."

Sam waved to Cholo to come meet them. "A little overwatch on the street never hurts," Sam explained. "I have some things to attend to here in the Old City. The car is yours as long as you like. Cholo will take care of you and anything you need. He understands English perfectly, but don't expect him to speak it. He doesn't much care for gringos."

"And you, Sam? His boss? He works for a gringo," Broadstreet teased.

"Only half gringo, Carleton. And sometimes that half doesn't show," Sam grinned.

Cholo caught Sam's attention as Broadstreet got into the car. He pulled down the corner of one eye, then held up two fingers making a walking motion with them before he jerked his thumb over his shoulder, pointing back down the street. *Two men, watching. On foot.*

Sam nodded in understanding and said, "Conduces el señor a la oficina y despues, al palacio del gobernador." He was directing Cholo to take Broadstreet to the office and later, to the governor's mansion.

"Claro, jefe. Nececitas pistola?" Cholo asked.

Sam shook his head, "La tengo."

"Entonces, cuidadte," the Panamanian driver warned. Just as Sam took care of Carlton Broadstreet, Cholo took care of Sam. If Sam had not already been armed, Cholo would have remedied the situation. Cholo would always remind Sam to be careful whether Sam needed reminding or not.

Sam looked over at Broadstreet, who was already settled in the car. "Marta will help you with anything you need in the office."

"Thank you, Sam. See you this evening."

Sam banged the roof of the car lightly with his hand and called, "Vaya!"

As the car pulled away, Sam headed back up the street, swinging his stick, in the direction where Cholo had seen the two men. He spotted them easily: a watcher on either side of the street, each conspicuously trying to act as if he were doing nothing. As Sam advanced, the one closest to him turned to study a shop window. It was the opening Sam was waiting for. *Okay, boys, let's see what you've got.*

Sam stopped, snapped his fingers, and turned abruptly as though he had forgotten something. Retracing his steps, he hurried down a side street he had just passed. When the shop-window watcher turned again and didn't see Sam, he waved to his partner, signaling frantically to the alleyway Sam had taken.

Sam made no effort to lose the men. In fact, he did just the opposite. His intent at this time was to find out if there were indeed only two of them. Normal operating procedure for street surveillance called for three tails. And if it had been a really serious shadow job, there would be multiples of three, along with teams in cars roaming ahead and behind to cover the flanking streets.

But I don't think that's the case here, Sam thought. *This feels more like someone just keeping tabs. Perhaps my friends over in Panamanian intel. But it's always best to know.*

Sam dawdled at the end of the block until he was sure the lads had him in sight again. Then he turned another corner and quickly crossed Avenida A. The two watchers made a mistake when they crossed behind and both ended up on the same side of the street as Sam. So he slowed again to see if he could spot a third tail on the other side of the avenue, but no one popped out.

I can't be sure yet, but I think it's only the two of them. And if so, that was a rookie play when they both crossed over to this side.

Now it was time to play cat and mouse in earnest. Sam stopped to buy a lottery ticket from a street vendor—a tiny, shriveled, crone that Sam and everyone else on the streets of Casco Viejo knew as La Bruja—the Witch.

He took his time selecting his ticket from the wooden rack propped on an easel next to the folding chair the old lady was perched on. When he handed her some money, he asked her if she knew the two young men following him.

"Oye, abuela. Alla atras, me sigien dos chicos. Ya, estan parada cerca a la esquina, mirando en este direcion. Los habia visto antes? Los conoces?"

As the old woman made change she cocked a rheumy eye in the direction Sam had pointed out. "Los veo," she rasped in a surprisingly strong voice. "Pero no los conozco. Aunque, a mi, se vean como maliantes."

Sam gently folded her delicate hand around the change she was about to give him. "Gracias, madre. Qué te quede el cambio," he told her.

"Qué te bendiga Dios, joven. Y no te preocupas de los dos pendejos, los regalaré del ojo malo," she said with a delighted cackle.

Sam tipped his hat to the old lady, gave the sidewalk pavement a quick tap with the tip of his cane, and continued down the street, enjoying the idea of La Bruja's "evil eye" working its magic on his inept young friends.

Further along he stopped and asked the time of an old gentleman. As he reset his watch, he caught a look at his pursuers. At the corner he started to get on a departing bus but when the tails panicked and came running, he waved it off and walked instead to a small city park across the way. He bought a newspaper from a street boy and sat at an open-air shoeshine stand tucked beneath the welcoming shade of a giant rubber tree. While the bootblack gave his shoes a thorough going over, Sam read his paper and kept a casual eye on his watchers as they hovered in the distance. They circled in a wide arc; first on one side, then the other, now and then crossing to the far side of the street.

These two boys are seriously lacking in tradecraft, Sam thought. *Whoever they work for should be ashamed to send out such an unprepared team.*

His shine finished, Sam paid and thanked the man. As he walked away, he put some coins in the can of a blind beggar sitting nearby. Then he looked around like a man undecided about where to go next. He patted his breast pockets as though looking for something—and coming up empty, made up his mind. Sam trotted across the street through a break in the traffic and made his way to a kiosk midway down the block, where he bought a cigar and chatted with the vendor for a few minutes. Lighting his cigar, he turned to make sure his tail was still with him. This time they hadn't spooked when he crossed the avenue.

Not bad, Sam thought, nodding his approval as he took a contented puff on his cigar. *One on this side, one on the other side. They've got me bracketed, ready for whichever way I may decide to go. They're catching on fast. But it's time to put an end to this game. Come on, boys, let's rumble.*

Sam turned to his left and moved out briskly. The man across the street waited until he was parallel with Sam and then fell into position slightly behind him. Sam paid no attention to the man on his side of the avenue, but he stopped at a jewelry shop and did a little window-shopping until the man could come closer. Then Sam set out again. He crossed to the next block and entered a men's haberdashery. He tried on a few hats and watched as first one, then the other tail made a pass by the storefront.

When he knew they were each farther down the block, Sam came out of the haberdashery shop and turned back in the other direction. Two doors back he slipped into an antiquities shop, a place owned by his dear friend Señora Vera Castillo, an elegant and wealthy widow from an old and very prominent Panamanian family.

Señora Castillo looked up with a delighted smile of recognition as Sam came in, but he gave her no time to speak as he moved past without stopping and said with a twinkle in his eye, "Holá, Vera. Disculpe la intrusion, pero estoy evitando a un marido enojado."

The woman knew Sam well enough to know his avoiding an angry husband was a very real possibility. She laughed and pointed toward the back door. "Entonces, Don Juan, apurete. Lo engañararé!"

Sam threw her a kiss over his shoulder and hustled out the back door into the alleyway behind. He then immediately entered the back entrance of the adjacent café and clicked the latch shut behind him.

Back out on the street, the watchers caught a flash of Sam's safari jacket on the way into the antiquities shop. The one on the near side of the boulevard strolled over and loitered nearby. After a minute he approached the door and, passing by, looked inside casually but failed to spy his quarry. He waited nervously for a half minute and then made a return pass by the storefront. Still nothing.

He waved to his partner, who scurried over to join him. After a short conference they finally decided they had no choice but to go in. First one, then the other entered the shop and looked around, appearing as out of place as they felt. Vera watched them with amusement.

"En qué puedo servirles, señores?" she asked, smiling, helpful, and sly.

One of the men, the older and more senior, stammered his question about the one-eyed man. “Un hombre—un tuerto, entró unos momentos antes. A donde fue?” he asked.

Vera pointed toward the back of the store and stepped aside as the men rushed for the back door. Outside, they stood in the trash-filled alley, making short forays in each direction, trying doors, scratching their heads, and cursing each other in frustration at having lost their quarry. After ranging the alley dejectedly, they left the way they had come.

In the café, Sam took a seat a few tables back from the window, where he could see the street but not be seen. A lovely young waitress came over to take his order. As she did, Sam looked at her with approval. She was a sturdy, well-built young woman. Her hair was done in two long, thick braids she wore wrapped around her head in a style still worn in the rural areas of the country. She had the looks and proud carriage, he thought, of a girl from the interior: Los Santos, Cocle, or maybe Veraguas province.

“Quiere el señor un menu?” she asked with a radiant smile.

“Solamente un cafecito, mi amor,” Sam replied. He couldn’t help it. Almost every woman was “his love,” one way or the other.

“A sus ordenes, caballero,” she said as she turned and hipped her way to the kitchen, playing to Sam’s audience of one.

He watched her go with genuine appreciation. *The women of Panamá,* he thought. *They are marvelous at all ages.* Then he sat back to smoke and watch the street.

He soon saw what he was expecting as his two watchers rushed onto the street, looking frantically in all directions. He got a close look at both of them as they paused to share thoughts outside his window. They were trim, lean-muscled young men; maybe early twenties, with intelligent faces. Neatly dressed in slacks and guayaberas. Sam thought they had the look of the city. They certainly weren't campesinos.

Okay, chicos. I won't forget either one of you, he thought, storing their faces away in his mind as he watched them hurry down the street still searching for their vanished quarry.

At that moment, the waitress returned with Sam's coffee. She leaned in to pour it and managed to strike just the right pose to give Sam a view of her ample cleavage.

"Su café, señor," she said, a coquettish lilt in her voice and a smile for his eye. She didn't spill a drop.

Sam played along. "Gracias, jovencita. Eres muy amable. Dime, cómo te llamas?" He asked.

"Lolita. My name is Lolita," she said, "I speak good Inglés," she added, putting the coffee down in some mysterious way that amplified the swell of her breasts.

Of course her name is Lolita, he thought. He stood up, grinning as he pulled out a chair for her. "Lolita is a lovely name. Tell me, Lolita, do you like to dance?"

Lolita slid into the chair, leaning forward, her lovely heart-shaped face cupped in her hands. Enchanted visions of swirling skirts in the moonlight were already dancing in her eyes. Sam felt his heart fill with wonder at how much he loved this country, this city, and these marvelous people.

SEIS

In the high-ceilinged, tile and stucco ballroom of the governor's palace, the whole of Panamá's diplomatic and social elite had gathered to welcome the new British ambassador and his wife. A pianist and small combo tucked away in a corner played safe—and boring—contemporary music. Waiters smoothed around the room with drinks and hors d'oeuvres while guests mingled and gossiped.

Carleton Broadstreet, drink in hand, chatted in a corner with his old friend, Francis Newcomer, a retired brigadier general and currently the governor of the Panamá Canal Zone.

"Quite a gathering, General. Looks like the who's who of Panamanian and diplomatic society," Carleton Broadstreet commented.

General Newcomer—most people still addressed him as general rather than governor—roamed the crowd with his eyes doing a head and quality count before responding, "I like to keep my finger on the pulse of things here, you know. Watch the cut and thrust of social intrigue. See who's riding a rising tide, who's becalmed, who's taking on water, and most important—who's going under."

Broadstreet took a sip of his drink and smiled. "From your choice of metaphors, one would think you had been an admiral rather than a general. But I take your drift to mean you keep a close eye on social and political goings-on."

"I do. Take that gentleman there, for example." Newcomer nodded toward a Panamanian man in his late middle years who was holding court with a group of admirers gathered in a tight cluster across the room.

"Arnulfo Arias. Fulfo, as he's popularly known. Been elected president of Panamá three times. Never served out a single term of office. You might remember we had him bounced during the war for flirting with the Nazis. Thought he could use Hitler to get a better treaty. All it got him was a quick trip back home to Penonomé. Same thing last year, his own people ousted him for corruption. We helped a little, of course. But he'll run again, I'm sure of it. And that young man at the edge of the group—the one who looks like a matinee idol? He is Jorge Villanueva, the current foreign minister. A fast-rising star in the government. Comes from a very wealthy family. Intelligent. Exceedingly well connected and politically gifted, he hates Americans with a visceral intensity. He'll make a run for the presidency when the time is right, I'm sure of it."

As though he knew he was being spoken of, Foreign Minister Villanueva looked over at Newcomer and dipped his chin in haughty recognition. Newcomer lifted his glass in salute and continued without pause. "But we'll thwart him when he does. Make no mistake about it."

"And the current president. Arosemena," Broadstreet asked. "What about him? What's your assessment?"

"Cut from the same cloth. But I understand your man is working with a view to easing him out if he proves too difficult. A clever young man you have there in Sammy Spears," the Canal Zone governor remarked approvingly.

"I understand you knew his father," Broadstreet mentioned.

"Oh yes. Very well. Knew him very well indeed. You might say he and I were the best of friends. Young in those days, of course. We arrived here together on the same ship back in 1909. So you might say I've known young Sam since he hatched from the egg. And just when you speak of the devil—there he is."

Newcomer waved with his cocktail toward the hallway. Broadstreet turned to see Sam as he entered, on his arm a stunningly beautiful woman dressed in a cream-colored, form-fitting gown perfectly complemented by pearl drop earrings and an opera-length strand of pearls glowing softly against her lustrous ebony skin.

"It seems she hangs upon the cheek of night like a rich jewel in an Ethiope's ear...except she is the Ethiope, of course. The snowy doves will turn green," the general said.

Sam, too, was well turned out for the gala in his ivory dinner jacket, white-on-white shirt, deep crimson bow tie with matching eye patch, and a sprig of Panamá rose looped into his buttonhole.

The sea of glittering politicos parted and hushed as the newly arrived couple made their entry. The buzz came alive and increased in excited volume in their wake when they recognized the tall, beautiful woman on Sam's arm.

The governor's wife herself rushed over to greet Sam and his date, taking them both by the arms and drawing them close. Melba Newcomer was a well-preserved matron in her mid-fifties with a cap of eternally blonde hair.

"Oh Sam!" Mrs. Newcomer remarked delightedly. "You are always so surprising!"

Sam gave her a peck on the cheek. "Melba, you know Alma, yes?"

Melba beamed, "Who *doesn't* know the famous Señorita Montera!"

Melba took Alma Montera's hand and gave it a warm, welcoming squeeze. "Thank you so much for coming, querida."

Alma gave the older woman a dazzling smile and embraced her closely. "What an honor, madame. I am so delighted to be here," Alma said in precise but heavily accented English.

Melba beamed at Miss Montera and turned to speak to Sam. "And thank you, Sam, for bringing her."

Sam grinned rakishly and replied, "The pleasure, I can assure you, is, and will be, all mine."

Sam winked as he and Alma shared a secret look that Melba pretended not to notice. She knew—and adored—her Sam. Instead, she took Alma by the elbow and led her into the center of the room. "Look everyone!" she announced brightly. "Miss Alma Montera!"

An excited crowd quickly gathered around the two women and all eyes were riveted on the grand lady Sam had escorted. Except for one person. And that person was not at all happy to see Sam Spears at the governor's party in the company of Señorita Alma Montera—or any other woman.

Across the room, Blanquita Villanueva had closely watched Sam's entrance. When she and Sam finally made eye contact, Blanquita looked disdainfully at Alma, now surrounded by admirers, and then pointedly back to Sam. She glared at him in naked displeasure. To which Sam only smiled and made a slight bow, which infuriated Señora Villanueva all the more.

Jorge Villanueva, both the Panamanian foreign minister and Blanquita's husband, caught the exchange. He looked coldly at his wife and fired heat in Sam's direction. Grabbing a drink from a passing waiter, he stalked woodenly outside to the veranda.

Sam watched Villanueva leave the room. He shrugged his shoulders to Blanquita as if to say, *Oh well. Husbands, you know,* and then ambled over to join Broadstreet and Newcomer, snagging a cocktail on his way.

"Gentlemen," Sam said, hoisting his glass to theirs with a nod of greeting as the three men touched glasses.

"Quite an entrance, my boy," Newcomer responded.

Sam looked over to see the crowd still clustered around his date. "Alma's the star; I'm merely her escort and driver."

"She is utterly stunning," Broadstreet remarked with evident appreciation. "But who is she?"

"Señorita Alma Montera. Shining star on the international music scene and Panamá's favorite daughter," the governor explained, admiration and pride in his voice.

Sam added, "She's the most renowned singer in Latin America. Bigger even than Agustín Lara was in his heyday."

Sam dropped his voice and continued. "And our biggest asset in the region. She's been courted and pursued by every president, politico, and business magnate from here to Mexico and back. She's just returned from a tour in Santo Domingo and has told me some very interesting tidbits about President Trujillo that I think we'll be able to put to great use."

Broadstreet gave Sam the smile of a doting father. "Ah, Sammy, Sammy. What a lovely web you do weave."

Sam returned the smile, touched his eye patch lightly, and lifted his glass in a toast. "For God and country."

The men chuckled together. "God and country," they pronounced as they joined the toast.

Governor Newcomer quickly became all business again. He took Sam by the elbow to lead him away. "Excuse us, Carleton. Sam hasn't met the ambassador yet."

"Of course," Broadstreet replied distractedly, turning his head to catch the passage of a particularly sultry and well-endowed young lady wearing a daringly low-cut gown.

As they crossed the room, Newcomer whispered to Sam in a voice notched a few decibels lower than his normal parade-ground roar.

"Want you to meet the guest of honor, Sam, His Britannic Majesty's newly appointed ambassador to the Republic of Panamá. They've sent us another one of their aristocratic drones. My God, they must have battalions of them over there! And a real poofter this time. Queer as a three-dollar bill and useless as tits on a boar hog. The Panamanians will love him."

Newcomer steered Sam to a small group clustered around the new British ambassador. A tall, gangly man in his late fifties, he was all elbows and sharp angles. He had a pinched, sour face, steep receding hairline, and from what Sam could hear four feet away, the standard drawn-out, condescending tones of an English aristocrat's upper-class public school accent.

Newcomer's towering presence cued the ambassador to turn toward and examine them down the length of his nose.

"Ambassador, may I introduce you to a particular friend of mine? Mr. Samuel Spears, please meet his Britannic Majesty's ambassador to Panamá, Lord Harrold Swathmore," Newcomer said. "Mr. Spears is the Canal Zone's liaison with La Guardia Nacional—Panamanian security."

Swathmore looked briefly at Newcomer as though trying to remember who he was, and then scrutinized Sam as though examining an unfamiliar species of insect. The ambassador did not extend his hand; he merely nodded his head. "How do you do," Swathmore, said. Perfunctory. Dismissive.

Noting the small slight, Sam touched his waist in lieu of a bow and said, "I'm pleased to meet you, Lord Swathmore. Welcome to Panamá."

Across the room, the ambassador's younger wife stood chatting absently with a group of women gathered about Melba Newcomer. Lady Felicity Swathmore was tall, with ash-blonde hair cut to her shoulders, and glowed with life and vitality. A man across the room caught her attention. A tall man with broad shoulders and the trim waist of an athlete. When he turned in profile she saw a crimson patch over his left eye. Felicity took a pensive sip of her drink, touched Melba on the forearm to get her attention, and nodded toward the group of men arrayed about the ambassador.

"Over there," she said, "Who is that dangerously delicious man?"

Melba knew instantly which man she was referring to. "The one with the eye patch?" she asked. "Is that who you mean?"

"Oh yes. The pirate. Who is he?" Lady Felicity said. Her voice had a throaty husk to it that was unmistakable.

Melba Newcomer could see the look in the younger woman's eyes and did not fail to recognize the meaning in her voice. She sighed to herself with a sense of resignation. *Oh goodness. Here we go again,* she thought, before replying, "That, Lady Swathmore, is my godson, Samuel Ransom Spears. May I introduce you?"

Felicity Swathmore blew a warm breath over the rim of her glass and replied softly, "Oh, thank you, Mrs. Newcomer, but not just yet. I wish, first, to savor him from a distance."

Melba sighed. She had seen this happen time and again and she knew, without a single doubt, that it was unlikely any good would come of it. But she also knew there was little she could do to intervene—even if she tried. Her Sam had that effect on women. He'd had that effect on her all his life, in a motherly sort of way, of course. And she was secretly more than a little proud of his charm.

So she merely smiled at Lady Swathmore with understanding and shook her head before slipping away to speak with some other guests.

Felicity never felt Melba leave. She had her eyes fixed on Sam. *Such a lean man,* she thought. *With an ivory dinner jacket cut perfectly for his broad shoulders and narrow waist. And that crimson eye patch!*

Sam felt the look and cast his eye to find its source. He and Felicity met eyes and exchanged a smile before Sam turned his attention back to Lord Swathmore, who continued to ignore Sam as he delivered a pedantic lecture to Governor Newcomer.

"Governor, my good man, as I was saying earlier, what's required here is greater Anglo-American cooperation in the canal administration. You must admit that we British know quite a lot about running a canal. Take Suez as the perfect example."

Sam took that opportunity to slip discretely away, ignoring Governor Newcomer's coughed "*Deserter*" as he did.

Sam wended his way through the crowd, stopping here and there for a few minutes at a time to speak with acquaintances, old friends, and an enemy or two. He finally landed at his objective point: the bar.

When Lady Felicity determined his destination, she decided it was the perfect place to zero in on him. As Sam stepped up to the gleaming carved mahogany bar and put his foot on its brass rail, Lady Felicity made her way across the floor of the ballroom.

The bartender, a San Blas Kuna Indian named Polo, was a fixture at the governor's mansion. Sam had known the man ever since he was a child visiting here with his father before the war. In those days Polo had been head groundskeeper. He later became the night guard. And now, in his later years, he was the majordomo of the mansion. Only for occasions such as this, when protocol and politics mixed like rum and Coke, would he manage the bar. Everyone in the hierarchy of the Canal Zone and the diplomatic corps of Panamá knew Polo. But only a very few, Sam among them, could call him a friend.

"Holá, maestro," Sam said in greeting. "Un Salvador Libre a favor."

"Cómo no, joven," Polo responded as he briefly touched Sam's palm with his own.

As Polo busied himself making the drink, Sam turned, elbows on the bar, to survey the room. Felicity Swathmore slid into position on what she assumed was his blind side—with the crimson eye patch. Sam Spears had no blind side. Especially when it came to women wearing Shalimar.

"What was that? The drink you ordered, I mean?" Felicity asked from Sam's elbow.

As he turned to her, Polo handed over his drink. Sam gave Felicity a look of good humor and lifted his drink up for view. "Salvador Libre," he said with a smile in his voice. "The Cuba Libre, as all the world knows, is rum and Coke. The Salvador Libre is rum and tonic with a slice of lime. I also like mine with a splash of bitter orange."

Felicity extended her hand. Her fingers were long and slender. "May I?" she asked, holding Sam's eye with hers.

He inclined his head and handed Felicity the glass. She never took her eyes off Sam's as she rolled the drink around in her mouth. "Ohhh, that's delicious," she purred. "And to think, I had to come all the way to Panama for the experience."

She returned Sam's glass, now blessed with a generous lipstick imprint on the rim. Sam accepted the glass and glancing over, spoke to Polo, who had been watching the exchange from the corner of his eye. "Una otra, maestro, para la señora."

Turning back again, Sam bowed slightly and said, "Samuel Spears, madam, or simply, Sam. And you are...?

Polo put the drink on the bar and spoke to Felicity but looked at Sam, "Su coktele, señora."

Felicity picked up the cocktail glass and lifted it to Sam with a salute. "Felicity Swathmore," she said. Steady.

"Ah, Lady Swathmore, the guest of honor," Sam said. "This is indeed a delight. Welcome to Panamá."

"Thank you, Mr. Spears," Felicity replied as the crystal of their glasses chimed. Steady. She drank.

"Please, call me Sam. My father was Mr. Spears." As Sam started to drink, he paused to turn the glass so he would raise the lipstick print to his mouth. Without taking his eye off Felicity's face, he put his lips on her lipstick print and then drank. He closed his eyes in satisfaction for just a second and smiled at her.

"Sam it is." Felicity felt an electric thrill course through her being and didn't trust herself to speak again for a few seconds.

So she drank and watched Sam over the rim of her glass. Then she asked, "Well, you know who I am. But tell me, who is Samuel Spears?"

"Like all the rest of the Zonies, Lady Swathmore, I help keep the canal doing what it does."

"Zonie? Remember I just arrived. I'm unfamiliar with the term. Just what exactly is a Zonie?"

"A Zonie," Sam said, "is a gringo, an American, who is a resident of the Panamá Canal Zone. Hence the word: Zonie."

"And just what do you do here, Sam?"

"I'm another interchangeable part; a functionary, a cog, in the great canal mechanism. In my case I function as the liaison between the Canal Zone Police and the Panamanian security officials—La Guardia Nacional. Mostly, I attempt to smooth over the inevitable bumps in the relationship."

Felicity lowered her voice to its most seductive. "No, what I really mean is, what do you *like* to do here? What is it that fires your blood? Stirs your passions?"

The combo, under prodding by Melba Newcomer, had finally livened up and a few couples had begun to dance. Sam put down his drink and offered his hand. "Shall we?" he asked with an inviting smile.

Felicity put her drink on the bar, nodded yes, and took Sam's hand. As they stepped onto the floor, Felicity was not surprised to find that Sam was a fluent dancer. She let her body move in unconscious rhythm to the music and Sam's light guidance. *This is like floating,* she thought, as they glided smoothly across the floor.

After a bit Felicity lifted her face to look at Sam. "My question was, what stirs your passions?"

Sam glanced down at the woman in his arms. He had expected her to be soft but he'd felt real strength in her supple athlete's body. "My passions," he said and wrinkled his brows. "I don't think I've ever been asked that question before. In fact, I'm sure I've never given it much thought."

"Yes, your passions, Sam. Your top three—in ascending order. Name them for me if you will."

"Well, let's see. There's big game fishing—especially for marlin," he said as he led her through a turn on the floor.

"That's one," she counted. "What else?"

"Then there's horse racing, of course."

"That makes two. And your favorite?"

Sam scanned her face before answering, learning every feature. The faint spray of freckles across the bridge of her nose, a few scattered dark flecks in her irises, the small scar over her right eyebrow, the high cheekbones, and the light dimple in her chin.

"My favorite?" he said at last. "The one passion that ranks above all others?"

"Yes, Sam, your favorite one of all," she said, her eyes exploring the rugged angles of his face. "The passion that drives you more than all else. Tell me what that is."

"It's very simple," he said, his eye crinkling at the corners as he grinned. "More than anything else, I love sleeping with other men's women."

Rather than a glare and a harsh rebuke, Felicity closed her eyes, threw back her head, and launched a full-throated guffaw. She absolutely shook with laughter, almost to the point of collapsing with mirth. She was so stricken she had to drape her arms across Sam's shoulders for support. People nearby turned to look—including Lord Swathmore, who gave his wife a disapproving frown. Sam gave everyone a smile and a shrug as he effortlessly took her weight and steered her to another corner of the floor.

"Oh goody!" she sobbed, wiping her eyes when she could contain herself and speak again. "Two of my favorite pastimes!"

Sam gave her a wry look. "Then I take it, madam, you do not fish?"

She threw a hand over her mouth to stifle another outburst. Then: "Not yet. But perhaps you could teach me," she said before sagging into him with another fit of the giggles.

Sam patted her gently on the back to help her quiet down and said, "It would give me, madam, the greatest of pleasure."

Felicity Swathmore looked at Sam with dancing eyes and said, "As it would I, dear sir. As it would I."

The song came to an end. Sam and Felicity joined in the polite applause. Sam took a card from his pocket and placed it in her hand. "I'd be glad to show you the sights sometime, Felicity—if I may."

She glanced at the card before tucking it away. "I'd like that. Thank you, Sam. I'm very glad we've met."

Lord Swathmore interrupted them to reclaim his property. Giving Sam his best stiff upper lip, he spoke to his wife. "Darling, I'd like you to meet the French ambassador. I need you to translate. The wretched man speaks not the first word of English."

Sam gave Felicity a small bow, took her hand, and brushed it with his lips. "Lady Swathmore, it has been a delight."

"Mr. Spears," she replied. "It has been a grand pleasure. I do hope we meet again."

Sam turned to Lord Swathmore. "And again, welcome, sir."

"Yesssss," Swathmore replied as he took his wife firmly by the arm and led her away. Felicity glanced back over her shoulder at Sam and mouthed, *I'll call.*

"Pardon? What was that?" Sam asked.

"For that tour, I'll give you a call."

"I look forward to it."

Sam was watching the elegant sway of her slim hips as she walked away when Melba tapped him on the shoulder, holding Alma by the hand. "Sam, can you get Alma to sing for us—just one song? She's refused me."

Several nearby couples chimed in. "Yes, a song. Please, Alma, give us a song!"

Alma Montero held a hand around her throat and tried to beg off. "But I am so tired from my trip. My voice is not good, and I don't want to disappoint."

Melba implored, "Darling, you could never disappoint. And it would be such a—"

Sam spoke up. "Mi, amor, why not a short one? Perhaps the one you taught me on the way over?"

Alma gave in to Sam with a challenging smile. "Only if you accompany me, Sam. If you play piano, I will sing."

"For you, mi cariña, I will attempt anything," Sam agreed, kissing her fingertips as he led her to the Rosewood Steinway grand piano in the alcove of the ballroom.

The hand-painted fifty-year-old piano was royalty in its own right: "King's Love" had been the governor's wedding gift to Melba, and she treasured it above all her earthly possessions. A master artist had painted the case in the late 1800s with romantic pastoral scenes and delicate gold tendrils. Sam had learned to play on this piano. He loved its rainbow of sublime tones.

Melba clapped her hands for attention and called excitedly to the room. "What a treat, everyone! Miss Alma Montera will sing for us!"

The room buzzed with delight, and there was a splatter of anticipatory applause. Sam sat at the piano and put his fingers on the ivory keys. Alma stood nearby and gave him a nod. Then, as Sam began the opening melancholy chords, Alma began singing in her husky contralto.

Alma played to the crowd, caught up in the music, and the shining cream gown caught her every movement. Sam looked up to see Felicity Swathmore staring at him, mesmerized, and he played only for her.

From the other side of the room, Blanquita Villanueva watched Sam and Felicity, her face darkening with mounting jealousy and anger. At Blanquita's side, her husband's face hardened into stone.

Alma brought the song to its crescendo, and Sam took it back down until it trailed to utter silence. He stood in the quiet, took Alma forward, and presented her to the room as the guests erupted in thunderous applause.

Felicity alone kept her eyes fixed on Sam as she clapped.

Sam scanned the room during the applause until he caught Felicity's eye and gave her a wink. Blanquita was watching, of course, and when Sam finally looked in her direction, she pegged him with a smoldering scowl. Melba had also been following the interchange among the three so she quickly stepped forward to kiss Alma on the cheek and lift her hand for a final round of applause, saying to the crowd, "Ladies and gentlemen, our own Miss Alma Montera!"

The applause rose again. As a crowd gathered around Alma, Melba Newcomer motioned to the combo to start up again and took Sam firmly by the arm and led him away. As they crossed the floor, she looked him in the eye and whispered, "Oh Sam. Whatever am I going to do with you?"

He adjusted his eye patch. "You could buy me a drink," he said with a boyish grin.

Melba shook her head and sighed, "I guess I'm getting off cheap."

As she led Sam to the bar, she looked discretely at Blanquita Villanueva. Melba leaned in close to Sam. She slapped him sharply on the backside and warned, "Stay out of trouble, Sam." She nodded toward the rapidly approaching Blanquita Villanueva. "Especially with that one," she said, before leaving him to his fate and joining her other guests.

Sam showed Polo two fingers. The barman slid a couple of drinks across the bar just as Blanquita stepped to Sam's side. Sam picked up his drink and indicated the other with a tip of his glass. "Join me, please, Señora Villanueva. Some party, don't you think?" He lifted his glass and took a sip.

Blanquita Villanueva tapped her gloved fingers on the bar and glanced at the waiting cocktail glass as though it contained poison.

"You make a fool of yourself!" she hissed. "First, by bringing that negra cantante to the reception, and now with your lewd attention to that puta Inglesa!"

Sam drank slowly and observed Blanquita over the rim of his glass. Her face was contorted in barely managed fury while Sam's was wreathed in a smile. He lowered his glass and bent his mouth to her ear.

"Jealousy becomes you, mi amor. It gives your face a particularly vivid coloration and yours eyes—Blanquita! They are simply aflame. I can't tell you how flattered I am that I can excite such emotions in you."

Blanquita clenched her fists and stamped a foot in anger. "Don't make fun of me, Sam Spears! Don't you *dare* make fun of me!"

Sam placed his drink on the bar and roamed the features of his lover's face. Her eyes darted over his also, taking in every crease, line, and angle.

Sam leaned closer and said with sincerity, "There are many things I love to do with you, querida Blanca. But making fun of you is not one of them."

She held Sam's look. The tension eased, her features softened, and looking down, she reached for the glass at her elbow and took a sip. Sam joined her. At last, she smiled.

"Okay, Sam. But sometimes—sometimes—you infuriate me like no other man has ever done."

"I can't deny, mi amor, that I do have my gifts," he said with a gleam in his eye.

Blanquita swatted him playfully on the arm. "Oh, tu eres un sin vergüenza, tu! No shame!" This time, they shared the laugh.

The evening was coming to a close. Guests had been departing around them. Jorge Villanueva came over to join them, stiff and formal. He gave Sam a curt nod and took his wife by the arm. "We must make our goodbyes to the governor and the ambassador, mi amor," he said.

Sam gave the foreign minister a nod in return, kissed Blanquita's gloved hand, and said, "Señor Ministro, Señora Villanueva, it was a great pleasure."

Villanueva stared at Sam impassively and said, "Igualmente, señor," before taking Blanquita a little too tightly by the arm and leading her away.

Sam watched them go and then joined Alma where she stood chatting with the Newcomers. "Quite the party, Melba," he said.

"Oh Sam! You and Miss Montera made it so!"

Alma gave the Newcomer's each a kiss on the cheek. "Thank you so much. It was a wonderful evening."

Melba gave her a kiss in return while a smile crossed the general's face and he unconsciously reached a hand to touch the spot where Alma's lips had touched his cheek. When he realized what he'd done, he dropped his hand like a schoolboy caught in a petty crime.

"Night, my boy, Miss Montera," he said, his face reddening slightly.

"Night, General. Melba, thank you. For everything," Sam replied as he kissed Melba and gave her the sprig of Panamá rose from his lapel.

"Buenas noches. Gracias por todos," Alma said, waving over her shoulder as she and Sam made for the door. Outside, they stopped for a second as Sam checked the fit of his eye patch and put on his hat.

At the end of the walkway, the Villanuevas were waiting for their car to arrive. Sam and Alma were walking by just as the car pulled to a stop, and two bodyguards jumped out to hold the doors for the couple to get in.

Sam and the guards made eye contact. Sam could see their startled looks as he passed beneath the light of the streetlamp.

Gotcha, pendejos, Sam thought with pleasure as he touched his hat in salute to the two men who had been tailing him that morning. *So you work for Villanueva, eh? How very interesting. But is it personal or professional, I wonder?*

As he and Alma kept walking, he heard the Packard's doors slam shut and the muted purr of the big V-8 engine as the sedan pulled away.

Sam and Alma arrived at his Ford Coupe. He opened her door and got her settled in, then walked to his side and climbed in. He turned on the engine, then draped an arm around her and asked the beautiful woman at his side, "Have a good time tonight?"

Alma slid closer to him and put a hand on his chest. "Yes, Sam. I did. But that man there, in the car. The Panamanian minister. All night he looks at you with hatred. Why?"

Sam shrugged. "I beat him once in a game of Chinese checkers. Perhaps it's that. I've always thought he's the kind of man that holds a grudge."

"Well, I don't like him—or his wife. I don't like the way she looks at you either," she said with a pout.

"Oh, forget them," he said, putting his finger under her chin and lifting her face to his. "So what now? Are you hungry? Would you like to go for a drink? Maybe to the yacht club?"

Alma Montera snuggled even closer to Sam, twining an arm in his and pressing a warm thigh against his leg. Putting her head on his shoulder, she spoke softly. "No drinks, Sam. Take me home. Show me how much you have missed me. Take *me* to paradise."

Sam leaned his face over hers, "Con mucho gusto, señorita—with the greatest of pleasure," he whispered.

Alma put her hand to the back of Sam's neck in a caress before pulling his face down to hers. Their lips met in a long, soulful kiss. When Sam came up again for air, he kissed her forehead. Alma tucked her head into his shoulder, left her hand on his thigh, and they drove away.

SIETE

Sam was in his office, kicked back at his desk, sipping coffee, and leafing through the morning newspapers: *La Prensa* and *El Diario*, two of the more sober Spanish language papers, and the *Star Herald* as the English language daily. Sam had them all spread out on the desk, comparing the front-page stories. All three carried the same headline:

UNIVERSITY CLOSED.
STUDENT LEADERS ARRESTED.
PUBLIC PROTEST OUTLAWED.

Sam took an appreciative sip of his dark roast coffee and said under his breath, "So, they finally took the bait. Bad move on Arosemena's part. That should really get things moving now."

Marta appeared at the door with some papers in her hand. Sam motioned to her. "Come in, Marta. What do you have there?"

Marta placed a short stack of papers on his desk and said, "These are supply orders and invoices for Contadora. And this," she said, handing him a small envelope, "someone slipped under the door—I think during the night. I found it only just now, where it had slid under the chair by my desk."

Sam took the envelope and looked it over, front and back. The only marking was a handwritten "SS" that looked like it had been hastily scribbled across the envelope's back seal. This served the purpose of showing that once sealed the envelope had not been reopened.

"Almost to your desk, huh. Whoever delivered it really shot it in, didn't they? Wanted to make sure it was all the way inside."

"It appears so, Samuel. Is there anything else?" Marta asked.

"Not this minute, love," he replied absently, holding the envelope to the light of the window. Marta left the room, leaving Sam alone at his desk.

Surprise was a staple of Sam's professional life, but the random occurrence of the unforeseen was a huge factor as well. Most of this Sam took in stride, but now and then something came up that caused his antennae to quiver and set off small alarms in his head. As he turned the envelope over in his hand and reread the initials penciled on the back, he knew this was one of those instances.

He put the envelope on the desk blotter and stared at it a few seconds before taking up a letter opener shaped like a small bayonet and neatly slicing it open along one side. He squeezed the envelope so that it opened wide, reached in with two fingers, and pulled out a doubled-over sheet of stationery. The note was printed in pencil with block letters.

"Must see you. *Urgent*. Will call," Sam read aloud, studying the note to see if he could recognize the printing. He refolded it along the crease lines and slid it back into its envelope. He started to lock it in a desk drawer, but then thought better of that and tucked the note into his shirt pocket.

He then went swiftly through the sheaf of papers Marta had brought him, signing those that required his endorsement and writing succinct replies to the rest. Paperwork finished for the time being, he rose from his desk, gathered up his hat, stick, and the signed papers, and headed out.

He placed the papers on Marta's desk as he went by and said, "I'll be out for a while, Marta, but I'll call periodically. If anyone comes in, have them wait for me, please, or get a number and location where I can reach them. And if Mr. Broadstreet calls or comes by, let him know I'll be back later this afternoon."

"Of course, Sam," she said. "And if I need to reach you?"

Sam checked his eye patch and the angle of his hat. "At the embassy for a while. After that, I'll call and let you know."

"Certainly, Samuel. Anything else?"

"Nothing that comes to mind just now. Gracias, mi amor."

Marta offered her cheek for Sam for a small kiss. When he had left, she sorted Sam's papers into different categories of action and attention. Marta had seen the envelope in Sam's shirt pocket and she, too, felt a slight tingle of unease. Not for the first time she sent up a silent prayer asking that Sam be protected.

* * * *

Lucius Merriweather looked as though he had been sent by central casting to play the role of a midlevel diplomat. He was tall and craggy, slightly stoop-shouldered, and had an intelligent face with keenly penetrating eyes shielded behind wire-rimmed glasses that were the height of fashion in 1930. He sported a neatly trimmed gray mustache and longish hair swept back from a high forehead. He was the very image of a career State Department professional. Merriweather was officially posted to the embassy in Panamá as the economics officer, but Sam knew, and appreciated him in, his true identity as an officer of the Bureau of Intelligence and Research, the State Department's intelligence arm. He was one of the truly great Latinists at State.

Merriweather had cut his teeth as a young foreign service officer in Mexico during that nation's murderous revolution. He had done extended tours in almost all of the banana republics of Central America. Two years in Spain during that country's civil war had honed his skills in undercover work. He had held an extended posting to Portugal running agents during World War II, and for half a decade after the war he was stationed in Havana. Now he was posted to Panamá, where he would serve out his last few years prior to retirement.

Sam considered Merriweather to be a friend and sometimes even an ally, but he knew him also as someone who didn't fully embrace the role of the upstart Central Intelligence Agency.

Merriweather closed the door to his office, motioned Sam to a comfortable armchair, and positioned his desk chair so he and Sam could sit facing one another. Then he fished an ancient briar pipe and a much-handled leather tobacco pouch from his jacket pocket and eyeballed Sam over the rim of those old wire-rims, packing his pipe.

"What brings you out this morning, Samuel? Haven't seen you in lo these many months." Merriweather spoke in the accent of a lifelong Boston Brahman.

Sam waited for him to apply match to bowl and get the pipe drawing properly before answering. "I didn't see you at the governor's gathering last evening, Lucius. I was a bit surprised you weren't there, given the reason for the occasion and all."

Merriweather puffed contentedly on his pipe. He studied Sam with a look that was focused but not unfriendly. At last he pushed a dense stream of smoke from the corner of his mouth and lowered his pipe. "The diplomatic community, such as it is in this veritable Garden of Eden, have already made their welcoming overtures to His Britannic Majesty's representative to the Republic of Panamá, Lord Swathmore.

"He and our own fair ambassador, the Right Honorable John Cooper Wiley, blessed be his name, have broken bread together, sniffed one another's respective credentials, and sealed a pact of perpetual amity with the kiss of peace. Last evening's gauche festivities at the governor's mansion were the final greetings to be issued, as it were, by the lower orders of Isthmian officialdom. So, putting aside my absence; what can I do for you?"

Merriweather put his pipe back between his teeth and puffed in relaxed pleasure while waiting for Sam to get to the point of his visit. Sam let his host enjoy his pipe a bit longer before speaking again.

"In the diplomatic world, it is well known that Panamá is the place you send your lepers, your cripples, and your pariahs. It is *not* where one of the major world powers posts a treasured asset. Rather it's a place of exile for those who are out of favor or have been slow to get the message that it's time to retire. Present company excepted, of course," Sam said, with a narrow grin.

Merriweather nodded agreeably, pointing to Sam with the stem of his pipe. "Present company also excepted, of course."

"According to my reckoning, Swathmore has been in the diplomatic service for almost thirty years. He has never been stationed in Latin America," Sam continued. "So, why here and why now? It doesn't make a bit of sense."

Merriweather studied the toe of his daring two-tone wingtips as his foot bounced rhythmically over his crossed knee. He wrinkled his brow as he formed his thoughts. Looking up he asked, "What do you know of the English upper class? The ones who came of age during and immediately after the first war?"

"Very little, I must admit. I brushed elbows with a few of them during the war—officers on Wingate's staff in Burma, for the most part. Talented men, I thought. Good soldiers who knew their business," Sam replied.

Merriweather blew a languid cloud of smoke toward the ceiling and watched with fascination as it swirled away into the blades of the old-fashioned ceiling fan. When he spoke again, he finally dropped the bogus New England accent and reverted to the crisp twang of his native Indiana.

"There are those kind, to be sure," he said. "Men who went out with the best intentions of serving the British Empire. Men like the ones you met, who put themselves in harm's way in some of the most dangerous and difficult assignments imaginable. True believers, you might call them."

He paused to take a few more thoughtful pulls on his pipe. "But there's another type also. The man of conscience who felt that his own peers—the ruling elite, the old order—were the ones responsible for the carnage of the first war. And believing England to be morally and politically bankrupt now, that type of man looked elsewhere for guidance with a view to creating a new social order."

"To Moscow, you mean," Sam suggested.

"To Moscow," Merriweather agreed. "These were young members of the intelligentsia who wished to bring about a radical change in British society. Some worked overtly toward that end, while others took a more clandestine route. Many of them entered government service to better influence the course of events."

"Are you saying that Swathmore is one of the latter?" Sam asked.

Lucius Merriweather sat quietly, absently tapping a forefinger on the arm of his chair. Suddenly he rose. Stepping to his desk, he unplugged the office intercom and disconnected the phone line from the wall. He returned to his chair, crossed his legs, studied his shoes again, and smoked in silence.

"You are aware, I'm sure, of the McCarthy hearings in the Senate and the inquiries of the House Un-American Activities Committee," he said.

"I am, Lucius. And I'm also aware it's had a devastating effect on the State Department."

"True. It has. A lot of good people, innocent people, have been caught up in the hysteria. But at the same time, a few rotten apples *have* been removed from the barrel. But that's the nature of purges and inquisitions. They turn up a few of the guilty but create a tremendous amount of damage once the process gets out of hand. During the thirties, the Spanish turned it into an art form."

"I agree, Lucius. But what does that have to do with my question about Lord Swathmore?"

"No one in the West has beaten the anti-communist drum with greater gusto than Churchill. I mean, my God! He coined the term 'Iron Curtain.' But have you noticed, Sam, that the Brits have never succumbed to the anti-communist hysteria that has consumed us these last few years?"

"I've never thought of it before, but now that you mention it—there's tremendous irony there. Forgive the pun. The hysteria is conspicuous by its absence."

"Do you wonder why?" Merriweather prodded.

Sam touched the corner of his eye patch, his unconscious tic of thought or concern. "Again, I've never thought about this until right now. But I suspect there must be a reason."

"There is. The Brits, those of the ruling class, are loath to investigate one of their own. To even form the concept that a member of the upper class *could*, much less *would*, betray his own race is an idea that can't be faced. And certainly not faced in public."

"So if there were suspicion of disloyalty, one might move that person to a place where they could do little or no harm—is that it?" Sam asked.

Merriweather smiled at Sam as if he were a precocious nephew who had just said something clever. "Seems to be the favored method. As you said, Panamá is the graveyard of diplomatic careers. Come here for a year or so, tack the title 'ambassador' to your many accolades, and as quickly as possible retire to life on the diplomatic has-been cocktail circuit."

"So what was the transgression?" Sam asked. "What did he do, or what has he been doing, that sent him here?"

Merriweather puffed again, this time attempting smoke rings, before answering. "Since shortly after the close of the war, Swathmore has been chargé d'affaires at the British embassy in Washington. There he was particularly close to an old school chum stationed as first secretary, a certain Kim Philby."

"Good God, Lucius! The one MI6 dismissed as a possible Soviet agent? That Kim Philby?"

"The same. There is conjecture that Swathmore and Philby had been lovers while at university together—not that the Brits would've cared one whit about that, but the two men have certainly maintained a close relationship over the years. So, when two other Brits—Burgess and Maclean, also Philby confederates—both fled last year to the Soviet Union, it was felt that Lord Swathmore's services were needed in a less critical post. A place where he could do less damage if it proves true that he's playing for the other side. After a year or two of quiet service here, he'll be replaced by someone equally mediocre and go quietly into retirement."

Merriweather's assessment was all the more chilling because it was likely to be true.

"Don't the British know that the Russians are doing their level best to get a foothold here?" Sam asked.

"I think our British cousins consider that to be our problem, not theirs."

Now it was time for Sam to sit back and connect the dots. *The war guilt clause at Versailles,* he thought. *Then the politics of revenge. Then Hiroshima. Now, la guerre froide. The Cold War. And the Brits think that virus won't spread.*

Merriweather smoked, watched Sam's face, and waited.

"You say he favors boys?" Sam asked. If Merriweather was surprised by the shift in conversation, he didn't show it.

"That's the word, Sam. Whatever that signifies. There's an old saying that an English lord would mount a goose if someone would hold its head. For people of Swathmore's class and standing, things of that nature are either pointedly ignored or quietly swept under the rug."

"It could explain some things, though," Sam said.

"If you're referring to the young wife, you may be correct. Or has this line of inquiry been about Her Ladyship all along?" Merriweather asked, peering inquisitively over the top of his glasses.

Sam smiled and then laughed. "A little bird of yours posted at last night's gathering, Lucius?"

"Your gallant attentions to the Lady have been noted and remarked upon in a number of circles around the city," Merriweather answered with a chuckle. "Radio Labio is swift, if not always sure."

Sam laughed as he thought of what Lucius had just said. Radio Labio—Lip Radio—was the term for how gossip spread so rapidly in Panamá.

Merriweather spread his hands to indicate his innocence in the matter. "Tongues love to wag, Sam. Those of us who know you are fully aware of your gracious and welcoming manner," he said with a smile. "Especially so when it comes to young ladies of the lovelier sort."

Sam stood to take his leave. "Lucius, it's heartening to know my labors in the vineyard have not been in vain. But now, which of us, do you think, should keep an eye on His Lordship?" he asked.

Merriweather rose also. "Since I'm the one with the little bird in the British nest, why don't I handle that task? I'll share with you any news that may be of significance."

"That sounds reasonable."

"And of course, you would not be loath to pass along any tidbits of interest you might possibly gather from conversation with Her Ladyship?"

"That's assuming, Lucius, there will be conversation."

Merriweather's eyes danced with mirth and something else: perhaps a touch of envy. He shook his head and said, "Ah, to be young again, Sam—you don't know what I'd give. To even think about the idea of pillow talk with such a beautiful young woman..." he looked Sam straight in the eye, delivering his line theatrically, "I'd give up my left eye."

Sam put two fingers to his eye patch in salute and laughed. "That would be a high price to pay, Lucius, but I have to agree—sometimes this seems to be worth it."

"One more thing before you're off," Merriweather added. "Have you heard any recent information about the Soviet's negotiations to put an office of their maritime bureau here in Panamá?"

"What little I know is that they have entered into discussions with the foreign minister's office. Villanueva's been playing coy with them," Sam said. "The Russians have no idea who they are dealing with. The Panamanians will milk them for all it's worth and then still not commit."

"True, very true. Panamá still hasn't recognized the Soviet Union. Hence no embassy, and hence, no intelligence agents here under diplomatic cover. But that would have to change with the establishment of a maritime affairs office," Merriweather said.

"I think we can preclude that from ever happening, Lucius. Much as Panamá would like a counterweight to our presence here, the main political parties—and especially the business community—are utterly against rolling out the welcome mat for the Russians."

"But what about your friends in La Guardia, Sam? Where do you think they stand on this?"

Sam didn't hesitate. "There may be some younger officers who would like to see a deal with the Russians. They'd enjoy thumbing their noses at the gringos. But the commander, Colonel Remón, is dead set against the idea. And if my sources are correct, Remón is seriously considering a run for president in this year's elections."

Merriweather's eyebrows shot up in surprise. "That's news to me, Sam. Are you confident of your sources?"

"I am. Very confident."

"So he intends to resign his command and run as a civilian?"

"Yes, like Somoza has done in Nicaragua. He'll take off the uniform and put on the business suit. The bankers and most of the merchant class are behind him; the church too. The main opposition will come from the old families who've always held the presidency, just rotated it among themselves, and see it as their birthright."

Merriweather's pipe had gone out in the ashtray on his desk. He headed back to clean and repack it. Sam coveted that ashtray as he always did. It was from the Tropicana in Havana. A simple-enough souvenir. But to the cognoscenti, it signaled the rise of Batista, the hedonism of the world's elite, and growing corruption by the Mafia. Lucius Merriweather, with his old-fashioned wire-rims and tropical wingtips, had been in the middle of all that.

"But if he wins," Merriweather asked, "can we control him?"

"He hungers for wealth, Lucius. He's seen what Batista in Cuba and Somoza in Nicaragua have been able to pile up with our help. He'll stay happily in the fold in exchange for our backing and a fat bank account."

"And then you can quit playing patty-cake with the leftists of the Student Union, is that so, Sam?" Merriweather put the question with a straight face.

Sam chuckled. "They serve their purpose, Lucius. Every day they're in the streets, they push the business community deeper into Colonel Remón's embrace."

"But today's papers say Arosemena has declared an emergency and outlawed public protest," he said.

Sam touched the side of his nose with a forefinger and winked. "Watch the news in the next few days. We may all be in for a surprise."

Merriweather extended his hand and smiled. "Go well, Sam. And be bold. The gods favor the bold. Careful and cautious is for cowards and shriveled old men like me."

Sam shook the older man's hand. "Thank you, Lucius. Your counsel, as always, has been invaluable."

After Sam left, Lucius Merriweather reconnected his phone and intercom. He settled himself comfortably in his padded desk chair and sat down, arranging a lined pad from the drawer and an old-fashioned inkwell just where he liked them. Looking at the fan lazily circling above his head to arrange his thoughts, he dipped the castle-shaped nib of his carved Spanish pen into the fresh pot of ink on his desk and began to write.

* * * *

When Sam left the embassy, he took a right onto Avenida Balboa and then a second right onto Calle 35. That was when he spotted the green Hudson Hornet in his rearview mirror, hovering just two cars behind him. The car had first caught his attention earlier that day. It stood out for two reasons. The Hornet itself was still so new, he just hadn't seen that many of them in Panamá. It was also beautifully designed and word was, it was fast. Not a car most men who loved cars would forget.

Sam kept the Hornet in sight as he made his way north through the city. But it veered off in a different direction when he headed into the Canal Zone, turning into the Curundu housing area.

Sam took the road that skirted the east side of Albrook Airfield and was waved through by the MPs as he entered Fort Clayton through the back gate. He cruised slowly and enjoyed the open, manicured spaciousness of the U.S. Army post that stood in contrast to the crowded chaos that was the norm just outside the gates.

But he had to admit—if forced to a choice between one side or the other, he preferred life on the Panamanian side of the fence. Orderliness had its attributes, he thought, but so, too, did the vibrant, disorderly, chaotic life in the Old City.

Sam slowed the Ford to a crawl when he soon met an infantry platoon marching in the opposite lane. Once past them, he turned right and took the road leading through a small neighborhood of family housing. He then turned right again along an almost forgotten road rimming the base of a hill from where he could see across the main barracks area and farther—across Gaillard Highway and beyond to Miraflores Locks.

It wasn't long before this brought him to the mouth of a narrow side street fairly overgrown with vegetation. Its mouth was marked by a faded sign that read, *ONE WAY, NO ENTRY*.

Sam ignored the sign, turned in, and began a steep climb. The path was completely roofed over by the jungle, a dark tunnel hidden from sight above and below, and ran straight uphill at a sharp incline. He downshifted to first and the V-8 engine growled in complaint as the craggy track carried him farther and farther upward through the dark pipeline of lush jungle foliage. Just after a stretch that seemed impossibly precipitous, he suddenly reached the summit and broke into a small clearing.

Sam parked his dusty Coupe on a small asphalt pad next to four other vehicles. He got out of the car and took a minute to look around. The open space comprised little more than half an acre, if that. The center of the flat hilltop supported a cluster of lofty antennas held securely in place by steel guy-wires embedded in concrete posts sunk deeply into the ground. A powerful diesel generator rumbled monotonously nearby in a metal-roofed concrete-block bunker. Across the clearing near the edge of the jungle stood four identical cast-concrete buildings. They were small and windowless, shaded only by the overhanging limbs of trees. In the center of each stood a single steel door.

Sam looked south. Through a gap in the tall trees he could see out over the mouth of the canal at La Boca, and farther, to Taboga and Taboguilla Islands. *It is so high here that if I had a pair of binoculars I believe I could see Contadora,* he thought as he walked to the nearest building.

At the door he took out a set of keys and, finding the correct one, inserted it into the lock. He held the doorknob in place as he gave the key a turn to the left, then back to the right, and finally left again. As tumblers retracted, the lock opened with a metallic *click*. From somewhere inside the building, he could hear a faint pulsing sound.

He stepped through the door. There was no light and the air was very cool. When he closed the door, he heard and felt the locking bolt fall back into place. Simultaneously a red light came on, giving him enough illumination to cross the barren room to a door set in the far wall. He selected another key from his ring and unlocked this interior door. As he stepped through it and onto a small landing, the door closed automatically behind him and another red lamp, fixed to the ceiling, came on. From this point, the only directional option was down.

Sam descended a metal stairway for two floors and arrived at yet another steel door; one with no handle or visible lock. On its frame was a small button similar to a doorbell. He hesitated, conjuring a memory, then tapped the button in a quick series of dots and dashes. He heard the soft snick of *yes* inside the door and it swung open, closing with a whoosh behind him.

He was suddenly in a large, bright room literally humming with activity. Along one wall, serious women wearing headsets sat in front of a bank of radio receivers. Mounted above each receiver sat the latest audiotape recording machines. Sam noticed a tape spool revolving on one machine now.

The next wall was completely taken up by a modern automatic telephone switchboard, and Sam knew there was another one just like it in the adjacent room. Along the third wall sat three other women, also wearing headsets, busily typing away as they transcribed conversations captured on the revolving spools of the tape recorders on the long wall shelf before them.

It was very cool in this subterranean room. In fact, it was almost cold, hence the light jackets and sweaters on the women. Sam knew this was one of the few air-conditioned structures in Panamá. He understood it wasn't for the comfort of the personnel: it was a requirement to keep the mass of electronic equipment from overheating. He had just about completed his scan of the room when a petite woman with heavy black-framed glasses, a thatch of short dark hair to match, and lively demeanor stepped briskly from behind a dividing wall to extend her hand in greeting.

"Samuel, welcome," she said, giving her wristwatch an approving glance. "I could set my watch by your arrival. You're always so punctual for our weekly séance."

Ilsa Matuzak spoke in precise American English but with the pronounced Central European accent of her native Czechoslovakia. During the war she had worked for the OSS, first as a radio signals intercept officer and translator in England and later as an agent parachuted behind German lines to set up communications networks for the anti-Nazi underground.

Sam considered her the best of the best when it came to signals intercept. At first he had been given a tough time prying her away from headquarters. But once convinced of the strategic value of this listening post, they had given him every support in getting Ilsa and her team up and running in this hidden dungeon atop a jungle-shrouded mountain, tucked far away in the back corner of nowhere.

"Mrs. Matuzak," Sam said as he took her hand, "I was—"

"Ilsa. Not Mrs. Matuzak. How many times must I tell you, Samuel? I am Ilsa," she interjected.

"Ilsa, yes," Sam replied with a smile. "It's not that I mean to be formal, Ilsa, it's just that *you* are the commander of the station here, and I always feel as though I should stand at attention when we speak."

The normally severe angles of Ilsa Matuzak's strong face softened as her mouth spread into a smile. "You flatter me, Samuel. But come, sit, and we will catch up on developments."

She took Sam by the elbow and guided him to a chair at a table placed precisely in the center of the room. The broad table served, Sam knew, as her desk, and literally, as the center of operations.

The two sat side by side, facing one another at a slight angle, their heads almost touching, so they could talk quietly and not disturb the equipment operators. Near Ilsa's right hand were several thick manila folders placed neatly atop the table. She passed Sam a single sheet of paper from the top of one folder, then took a cigarette from a pack of Gitanes on the desk and inserted it into a carved ivory cigarette holder that was yellowed with age.

She put her hand lightly on Sam's as he gave her a light with the battered Ronson lighter that had belonged to his father. She nodded her thanks and then, as she sat quietly smoking, Sam read over the week's summary report. When he had finished, he put the sheet squarely before him on the table and gave his attention back to the remarkable lady sitting at his elbow.

Sam said nothing. He just watched in fascination as Ilsa brought the cigarette holder to her lips. She smoked in the continental manner, eyes slightly closed, the cigarette holder clasped lightly between thumb and forefinger, with the palm of her hand toward her face. Sam thought such a theatrical style would appear a foolish affectation in anyone else, but with Ilsa, it was elegant and perfectly natural.

"So?" she asked, arching an eyebrow in inquiry. "What do you think?"

Sam arranged his thoughts, watching her smoke curl.

"How many of Villanueva's conversations with the Russians in their Mexico City embassy were placed from his home phone and *not* from the foreign ministry office?"

Ilsa lightly touched the tip of her cigarette to the rim of an ashtray and answered, "Four, Sam. He placed four of the calls from his home phone."

"And when did the calls commence? Before his trip to Mexico City or afterward?"

"After his return. Prior to his trip he made no calls from his home to the Soviet's Mexico embassy."

"Do we know who he spoke with?"

She nodded. "Oh yes. The calls were routed through the embassy switchboard to the office of the economic secretary, Anatoly Lavrov."

"And it was Lavrov Villanueva spoke with on each of the calls?"

"Yes. It was Lavrov on each occasion."

"You are certain of that?"

"Yes, Sam. We've identified him by voice."

"I'm certain Villanueva has no Russian. So, did they converse in English or Spanish?" Sam asked.

"In Spanish, always in Spanish. Lavrov's mother, you know, was from Spain and he lived there as a child. He speaks the language beautifully, but with a pronounced Castilian accent. I'm sure the Mexicans think him hugely pretentious." Ilsa seem amused by the idea of a Russian social elitist.

Sam absently prodded the fabric edge of his eye patch and then nodded toward the manila folders on the desk. "You've had all the conversations transcribed?"

"Yes, all transcribed, as is the norm," Ilsa said as solemn as an oath.

Sam looked closely at her and she returned his gaze with anticipation. He knew her mind was as keen as a New York deli meat slicer. For her part, Ilsa was aware that Sam valued her thoughts, and it always pleased her when he asked her opinion, as he did now.

"Why," Sam asked her, almost rhetorically, "would the Soviet economic secretary in Mexico City be having multiple, highly sensitive conversations with Panamá's foreign minister over an open telephone line? Surely he must know we're listening."

Ilsa pulled on her cigarette and studied its ivory holder before answering. "I would think," she said, exhaling a thin stream of smoke, "that Señor Villanueva is unaware we have tapped his home phone and thus he feels secure. And that Secretary Lavrov not only does not care that we are listening, but actually wishes us to be privy to what is transpiring."

Sam pointed to the pack of cigarettes. *May I,* his eyes asked. She slid the pack across and watched as Sam tapped the end of the cigarette against his thumbnail and flicked the Ronson to life and lit up. He inhaled deeply, feeling the rush of nicotine entering his system, and then spoke slowly and deliberately.

"Does the foreign ministry have a secure telex link to the Soviet embassy in Mexico City?"

"No, Sam. They do not."

"Do they have secure telex capability at all?"

"Not at all, Sam."

"Have they exchanged coded commercial telegrams with one another?"

"No, they have not."

"So the only other method of secure communication Villanueva could possibly have with Lavrov is via letter sent by diplomatic pouch to the Panamanian embassy in Mexico City and delivered by hand. Would you say that is correct?"

"That would be one way. The only other method would be to send it by personal messenger. Which, as we both know, is the most secure means of communication."

"And it appears Villanueva, in this matter, is his own messenger."

"We do not know for sure, but it appears that way."

"So once again. Why are they having an open conversation—open negotiations even—about establishing an office of the Soviet maritime bureau in Panamá?"

Ilsa explained. "Let's connect the dots. The Russians haven't sent commercial traffic through the canal since the war. But when they do, they will have to contract through a third-party broker to facilitate transit of their merchant vessels. That costs hard currency—dollars—they hate to part with. You know what notorious cheapskates the Russians are. Also, they will not want anyone looking closely at bills of lading. So, opening an office in Panamá to process their own shipping makes sense—especially if it can be done openly and aboveboard. It also informs us that we have no say-so in the matter. The United States told the Russians they can't have an office in the Canal Zone. So this workaround gives them one on sovereign Panamanian territory."

"Exactly so, Ilsa. We can grumble about it, but that's about all we can do. But maybe this is only a ruse, a red herring to capture our attention while something else, something genuinely hidden, is going on. What do you think?"

Ilsa stubbed out her cigarette and looked at him. "Perhaps the answer is to be found on the Russian trawler sitting offshore just outside the international boundary."

Surprised now, Sam asked, "Have we been picking up transmissions from them?"

Ilsa nodded and touched one of the manila folders. "We have, but they're not using normal code. I think they are using one-time pads or book code."

Sam drummed his fingers on the table and said thoughtfully, "Agents use one-time pads and book code."

Ilsa nodded her agreement. "That is so."

"Has there been a response from shore?" he asked.

She frowned. "That's what is so puzzling, Samuel. The transmissions have been very short. They seem to be announcements—perhaps something such as 'we are here.' Or they could be prearranged signals that set an act in motion but require no response, much along the lines of BBC broadcasts during the war to agents in Europe. Even if decoded, the message would probably say something nonsensical like, 'I have a lovely bunch of coconuts.' Only the intended recipient would know the real meaning of the message," she concluded with consternation.

Sam's brows furrowed and he said, "So a reply could be hidden in the same manner, say, in a certain song at a certain time of day from one of the commercial radio stations."

"Yes, that's a possibility. Another is that if a transmitter on shore knew the location of the ship beforehand, and made use of a directional antennae, it would be very difficult to detect a response."

"You would have to be in line with the transmission to pick it up?" Sam asked.

Ilsa nodded again. "Within say, ten to fifteen degrees, depending on the configuration and accuracy of the transmitting station's radiating wire."

"How did the Germans solve that problem?" he asked, stabbing out his cigarette in the ashtray.

"They used multiple intercept teams with equipment mounted in trucks. Each truck covered a certain arc of the target area. When they found a transmitter, they would keep refining the area until they had it down to a few square blocks in a city, or a couple of hectares in the countryside. Then they cordoned off the area and conducted a systematic search. They were, as you know, very thorough."

Sam knew Ilsa spoke from hard-won experience. She had almost been caught in just such a Gestapo sweep. She had left the attic where she kept a hidden transmitter only minutes before the Germans raided the building. As it was, she watched the raid from a café across the street. They found her equipment but nothing and no one else. But in their frustration at failing to bag the spy team, the Gestapo shot the owner of the building, Ilsa's friend, as a warning to others.

"So, without the proper equipment and teams, we would not be able to determine the location of a transmitter in the city, is that correct?"

Ilsa shook her head, causing her thick hair to bounce off her cheeks. "Again, Samuel, not if they are using a directional antennae. And you know how innocuous-looking that is: a single strand of wire, cut to a certain length according to the frequency used, and slanting down in the direction of the receiving station. It is child's play to put in place and almost impossible to detect. And there is something else that just came to me."

"Yes?" Sam asked with genuine interest.

"The transmitter need not be very powerful; five watts or less, which makes it even more difficult to detect."

Sam drummed his fingers on the table again as he absorbed this information. "Then all we can reasonably surmise is that the ship is communicating with someone on shore."

"Actually, Samuel, all we know for certain is that the ship is transmitting *apparent* messages in what *appears* to be a book code or is perhaps using a one-time pad. They could be doing nothing more than sending dummy messages just to keep us busy. They know for certain our navy has followed their progress down the coast and is listening intently to their every transmission. What we've picked up may be no more than their idea of a little joke."

Sam studied her closely and saw something in her eyes that matched his: a hunter's instinct. "But you don't believe that, do you?" he asked quietly.

Ilsa shook her head imperceptibly. "No, I do not. I can feel this. They are up to something."

Sam was struck by a sudden thought. He pointed to a map on the wall. "Where is the ship now? Do you have a good idea of their location?"

They both stood and walked over to the map.

"Cruising back and forth, here." Ilsa pointed to an area due south of the city and far out to sea. "Between Punta Mala at the tip of the Azuero Peninsula in the west," she pointed again. "And here. A position off the coast near the Colombian border in the east."

"Well south of the Perlas Islands, it appears," Sam noted.

"Yes, they have scrupulously avoided coming near Panamanian territorial waters," she said.

“What has the navy done? Are they shadowing the ship?”

“No longer. Not since they were off the coast of California. Since then they just listen and monitor their movements.”

Sam studied the map and the figure-eight pattern of the ship that Ilsa had described, and a thought came to him, but one he didn’t speak aloud.

Contadora Island would be in the line of radiation of any clandestine transmission from a station in the city. Or could the station not be in the city but on one of the many islands of the archipelago? Could it even be on Contadora itself?

Sam knew the answer to both questions. *Yes. It was possible.* But was it so? And that was the maddening part. He could not be sure if this was big and juicy or a big fat zero. However, his gut told him Ilsa was right. The Reds were definitely up to *something* here in Panamá.

Sam studied the map a minute longer before turning back to Ilsa Matuzak. “I always come away from our get-togethers with a full mind. You’ve given me much to think about, and it may take time to digest it all. But I agree with you: something is brewing here—something we need to get to the bottom of.”

Ilsa took Sam by the elbow and led him back to the table. “Yes, Samuel. Something. My team can only report what we pick up. The interpretation of that material is a province that belongs solely to you.”

At the desk again, she slid a sheet of paper from beneath one of the folders. She stepped close to Sam and said, handing him the paper, "We intercept only, and make no analysis, but I thought you would be interested to see this."

He looked at her quizzically as he took the sheet of paper. He began to read. After a few lines he stifled a chuckle and slanted his eyes at her. He finished reading and returned the paper to her.

Ilsa took the sheet, slid it back beneath a folder, and offered without looking up, "Samuel, you knew we were listening to the foreign minister's home phone. You must have known we would pick up *all* calls from there, both in and out."

Sam laughed. "Even the ones made to my home phone, you mean?"

Ilsa seemed embarrassed as she spoke. "Yes, even those." She looked up at him then and hurried to say, "I make no judgments—certainly not about your personal life. But as someone with experience of the world, as a woman myself, I feel compelled to tell you, be careful of her, Samuel. I've seen Señora Villanueva's type before, in many lands and in many guises. She is a dangerous woman. A very dangerous woman."

Sam almost laughed at this but caught himself when he saw the serious look on Ilsa's face.

"Ilsa, old friend, I appreciate your concern. I also appreciate the fact you made me aware of this. I can only offer you, and any of the ladies who took the calls and made the transcripts, my apologies for the embarrassment this may have caused."

Ilsa gave him a shy smile. "I am no prude, and neither are the other ladies—in fact, you are somewhat of a hero to several of them."

"Then make sure the transcripts stay part of the record. If I'm ever brought up on charges these may help with an insanity plea," he said with a large smile. "Now then, I need to call my office. May I use your phone?"

Ilsa pointed to the phone on her desk. "By all means. And you needn't worry about this one. Even if it were tapped it would show a number and a street address in Asbury Park, New Jersey."

"Then perhaps I may use this one for all my personal calls in the future," Sam said with a grin.

As Sam picked up the receiver and dialed the number for his office, Ilsa stepped to the other side of the room and spoke with one of the stenographers transcribing tapes.

Marta picked up on the second ring. "Holá, Marta, aqui habla Sam. Any calls I should know about?"

"A man called to say he had left you a previous message and that he would call again this afternoon," she said in a calm, businesslike voice, a tone Sam recognized as carrying a sense of urgency.

"Okay, mi amor. Are you going out for lunch today?" Sam asked. It was code for: *stay at your desk until I arrive.*

"Yes, I'm meeting my sister at Velario's at noon," she replied, which meant: *I won't budge until you return.*

"Okay, give Rosa my love. I'll see you later this afternoon."

Sam hung up. He knew from the sound of Marta's voice that the caller had probably given a time when he would call again, that the appointed hour was drawing near, and that Sam needed to hurry. He retrieved his hat and cane from the entry table where he had left them when he arrived. Ilsa saw that his call was finished and he was preparing to leave and came over. Sam extended his hand.

"Ilsa, my thanks to you and your team. You are all doing marvelous work. And if you have additional thoughts concerning these Russian transmissions, don't wait, but let me know immediately. We're missing something here, and I've a feeling it may be very important."

Ilsa gave Sam her hand. "Yes, of course. If anything occurs I'll be in contact straightaway." Ilsa placed her other hand over his and squeezed it lightly. "Go well, Samuel. I know better than to say, *be careful.*"

"Adios, Ilsa." With that and a small bow to his friend, Sam put on his hat, tapped his cane twice on the floor, and turned to make his way back aboveground. As he departed, several of the women glanced up from their work, discreet smiles on their lips, to watch him leave.

OCHO

When Sam left the listening post, he took as direct a route as possible back to his office. Once off the mountain, he made his way to the front gate of Fort Clayton and turned left onto Gaillard Highway, the main road through the Canal Zone. It brought him past Corozal, into the canal headquarters town of Balboa, and then back into Panamá City at the intersection with Avenida A. This took him through the wooden slums of El Chorillo and from there, the short distance into Panamá Viejo, the Old City.

As he drove, Sam followed the ancient military dictate to "make haste slowly." The Canal Zone Police were sticklers for enforcing the speed limit, and though Sam was immune from getting a citation for speeding, he didn't need the time-consuming nuisance of being pulled over. The same thing applied once he was back on the Panamanian side. He didn't want the impediment of having to deal with a dutiful traffic cop. As it was,

Sam drove at a steady but rapid pace that brought him to his office in twenty minutes. He backed in under the covered archway at the side of his building and parked.

At the rear of the parking area, Cholo was busy hosing the dust off the Willys. When he saw Sam, he pointed to the Ford and splashed a spray of water in that direction. Sam nodded yes and tossed him the keys. Cholo pocketed the keys and continued his chore as Sam went inside.

Marta was at her desk, typing. When Sam entered she stood and followed him into his office. Sam hung his hat and jacket on the rack and propped his stick in the corner. He pointed Marta to a chair and he sat on the edge of his desk. He adjusted the headband of his patch, lifted an eyebrow, and said, "Okay. Fill me in."

Sam could see Marta arranging her thoughts before she spoke, and then, when she did, it was all in complete and perfect order.

"First, Mr. Broadstreet sent you a message," she said as she handed him an open envelope, "to say he was leaving on the midday flight to Miami and that he would send you a response to your order once he was back at headquarters."

Sam glanced at the note before placing it on his desk. He was surprised at Broadstreet's abrupt departure but only mildly so. He knew Carleton had a lot on his plate that needed tending back in Washington. Sam didn't envy his boss's position or wish for his job. A tour of duty in the snake pit of Agency headquarters was Sam's idea of hell on earth.

"Then, a man called by phone, this morning at 10:03," Marta continued. "He spoke in English. An American, a young man, with no discernible regional accent." She paused to let Sam absorb the preliminary description. Sam nodded that she should go ahead.

"He asked if you had received his note. I told him that if it were he who had placed a note under the door that, yes, it had been received. He asked to speak with you and sounded agitated when I told him you were not in. I asked if I could take a message. He ignored my question and said he would call again at three thirty this afternoon. I told him I didn't know if you would be back at that time and asked again if I could take a message for you.

"He was quiet for several seconds. I could hear street sounds in the background, and I knew he was on the line still because I heard him sigh. When he spoke again, it sounded as though he had cupped his hand over the mouthpiece of the phone. He said quietly, but very distinctly, '*Tell him Kutasov was murdered.*' I tried to keep him on the line. I began to ask him to repeat what he had said but he hung up."

Marta sat quietly and waited, notepad in hand, ready to take notes or respond to Sam's questions. Sam deliberated, staring at the floor and drumming the desktop lightly.

"You say you heard street noises. Did it sound like he was calling from a phone box?"

Marta nodded in the affirmative. "Yes, Samuel. It had to have been a call from an outside phone."

Sam glanced at his watch. "It's ten till three; that gives us a little more than half an hour. Have we received any other calls since then?"

"Only yours, Samuel," she replied.

"Then we're in luck. Please call Ilsa Matuzak and ask if she can trace the source of that last call. Tell her it's urgent. We need it within the half hour."

Marta reached for the phone on Sam's desk and began to dial.

"After that, switch all incoming calls to my desk," Sam said as he slid around the desk to sit in his chair.

Marta nodded again to indicate her understanding. As she gave instructions for the phone trace, Sam leaned back in the chair and lit a cigar, determined to bide his time and wait patiently until three thirty.

At three sixteen, the phone rang. Sam picked up the receiver and said, "Yes?"

A woman's voice, but not Ilsa Matuzak's, said, "The call was placed from a public phone located on Calle D at the north side of Santa Ana Park. I say again, Calle D at Santa Ana Park."

Sam said, "Got it. Thank you."

He hung up and called out for Marta. She was at the door immediately. "Yes, Samuel?"

"Send Cholo to me, please," Sam ordered.

When he arrived, Sam gave the inscrutable Panamanian quick instructions in the verbal shorthand the two men had developed over many years together. Long explanations were seldom needed.

"Oye, hermano; del telefono publico en Calle D, al lado norte del Parque Santa Ana—a las tres y media, llamará un tipo, quizas un Americano," said Sam. "Sigalo despuese la llamada pa' confirmes a donde va, y si sea posible, en donde se queda. Me entiendes?"

Sam was assigning Cholo the task of overwatching the phone on Calle D and asking him to follow the man after he made his second call.

Cholo checked his watch. He was already calculating the distance to the location and the amount of time it would take him to get there. He repeated the location and time back to Sam: "Calle D, Parque Santa Ana, tres y media. Claro que sí."

With no need for further speech and little time to lose, Cholo turned and hurried from the room. Sam pulled the phone to the near edge of his desk. He would set up a meeting with this mystery caller and with luck, he thought, would have a report from Cholo beforehand. Sam checked his watch again: three fifteen. He sat back to wait.

Sam watched the minute hand on the wall clock as it clicked down to point directly at the numeral six. He kept his eye fixed on the clock as the minute hand continued its march: Three thirty-five. Three forty. Three forty-five.

By four o'clock, Sam was sure there would be no call. At four-fifteen, Cholo entered the office and stood silently in the doorway.

Sam looked up. "Anybody?" he asked.

Cholo lifted his hands to his side, palms out, and shook his head. "Ni cualquiera persona," he returned.

"Okay, mi hermano. Stick around. I may need you in a bit," Sam instructed.

"Estaré listo," Cholo answered and left the room.

Sam reached for the box on his desk and took out a cigar, but then thought better and put it back in the box. It wasn't a smoke he wanted, but answers.

Kutasov was murdered. It has to be someone from the island, he thought. *Or does it? Who else knew? Only a few people on Contadora were aware of the death. And fewer still knew a name. And off the island?*

Let's see, he thought. *Other than myself, there is Marta and Cholo—but even Cholo had not heard a name. Then, there was Father Mike, Lieutenant Gaddis—but no, it was unlikely the pilot knew anything; that left Carleton Broadstreet and the section at HQ that was in charge of the program. No, it's someone here. That much is obvious. But who could it be?*

An idea struck him. *Maybe,* he thought, *just maybe. It certainly bears checking out.*

Sam stepped to the door and spoke to Marta. "Would you send a message to Walter Driscoll and ask him if anyone from the island is here in the city, even if it's someone in transit in or out of the country?"

"Yes, Samuel, of course. Shall I encode the message?"

"Yes, standard code, please. Tell him I need an answer as soon as possible."

As Marta stepped to the closet that held the Teletype machine, Sam went to the hat rack just inside his office doorway. He reached into the breast pocket of his jacket and took out the envelope with the message inside. He returned to his chair, placed the envelope on the desk, and leaned forward to scrutinize it closely.

He studied the front of the envelope then turned it over to look at the back side. He detected nothing but the "SS" that was written in cursive across the seam of the flap. He felt sure he was the only person to have opened the envelope once it had been sealed. He held it to the light and turned it over in his hand, looking at it from different angles. He then ran his fingers over it to gauge the texture of the paper.

Inexpensive, he thought. *In fact, downright cheap. Ten cents a box at any stationary store, or the kind you find in the nightstand of any cheap...*

Sam quickly reached two fingers inside the envelope and plucked out the note. He spread it open on the desk and studied it minutely. *Must see you. Urgent. Will call.* The note was written in block letters with a dull pencil. The underlining of the word "urgent" was slightly smudged, as though the writer had made a miss-stroke with the pencil and had done it a second time. Sam picked the note up, and turning it side to side and back and forth, he eyed it at different angles. Then he held it up to the window for the light to shine through. *Ah! There,* he thought. *Maybe, just maybe!*

Sam spread the note flat on the desk blotter and took a new number two pencil from the center desk drawer. He stepped to the pencil sharpener mounted on the side of a wooden file cabinet and, taking his time, drew the nib of the pencil to a long, fine point. Back at his desk, he held the note pressed as flat as possible and, beginning at the top and working down, raked the side of the pencil point rapidly back and forth across the sheet of paper.

The graphite smeared across the paper, darkening it in wide overlapping swaths but leaving a barely discernable series of short lines in the midst of the broad smudge. Sam reached into the desk drawer and pulled out a heavy tortoise-handled magnifying glass. He held the glass over the sheet of paper and found the right focal distance.

There it is! Yes, there! The writing was faint but readable and also in block letters that seemed to match the style on the note. It read Hotel Corinto 34.

Hotel Corinto, Sam thought. *Isn't that a Casa de Citas—a no-tell hotel—that rents rooms by the hour? Yeah, that's it. It's above a bar called El Marinero over on Avenida Colón.*

Sam took his .32 automatic from the center desk drawer, checked to make sure a round was chambered, and tucked the pistol into his waistband. *You never know,* he thought as he also put a fully loaded spare magazine in his pocket. Then, quickly crossing the room, he grabbed his hat, jacket, and cane and was out the door.

* * * *

Cholo parked the car across the street and about three buildings down from El Marinero, where they could get a good look at the place. This was part of the sleaze district of the city. Cheap bars, cathouses, no-tell hotels, and all the assorted riff-raff and human flotsam and jetsam attracted to such a district. Even at this time of the day, there were a number of hookers working the street—mainly, the older, more broken-down and desperate ones.

Sam conferred with Cholo. "You go around to the alley and keep watch. If anybody runs out the back way, put them on the ground and hold them until I get there."

"Okay" was all Cholo said in reply.

"You have your pistol on you, yes?" Sam asked.

Cholo opened his jacket and turned toward Sam to show the big GI .45 he had in a shoulder holster beneath his left arm. Sam noticed the hammer was cocked and the safety catch was on.

Sam nodded and said, "Good. I'm not expecting trouble, but it's best to be ready."

The men got out and locked the doors to the car. A skinny, ragged boy sitting on the curb nearby was watching hungrily as they got out of the Ford. Cholo flipped the boy a fifty-cent piece and pointed to the Ford. The kid leaped to his feet and caught the coin deftly in midair. He gave Cholo a huge grin as he ran up and took up guard duty on the sidewalk by the driver's side of the car.

Cholo said over his shoulder as he walked away, "Una otra cuando regresa yo." Sam knew the kid would protect the car with his life in return for that silver fifty-cent piece now, and the promise of another soon to come.

Sam waited until he saw Cholo disappear around the corner before crossing the street. He picked his way carefully through the traffic and over the accumulated crud and ground-in debris that filled the gutters. The brilliant sun had dried the cast-out garbage, puddles of vomit, and other filth to a uniform dusty consistency, and the dry season trade winds swept away the stench.

It would take the return of the nine-month-long rainy season to flush the area clean. The rains weren't due again until April, and that was still three months away. But at least the business owners along the street kept the sidewalks splashed down and the dust swept away. At least most of them did; the exception was the four-story building that housed the El Marinero bar on the ground floor and the Hotel Corinto above.

Sam stood on the sidewalk and studied the front of the building. To the right was a narrow stairway that disappeared into darkness as it rose from street level to the floor above. A faded, traffic-grimed sign with an upward-pointing arrow showed the way to Hotel Corinto. To the left, trying hard to evoke the Old West, was the planked swinging door entrance to the bar. The sign hanging above the wooden door had a surprisingly well-painted picture of a sailor walking down a street with a pretty girl on his arm. Lettering on the front window pronounced the place as being El Bar Marinero.

Sam pushed one wing of the swinging door open with the tip of his cane and walked in. He stepped in and to the right of the door and waited for his eyes to adjust to the darkness inside. The place was little different than any number of dives in this part of the city. A long mahogany bar against the far wall fronted by battered stools, a scattering of mismatched chairs and tables, and three fans hanging from the pressed-tin ceiling—only one of which worked. There were maybe a half-dozen early patrons scattered around a room that could accommodate forty. Nothing had changed in the fifty years since the joint was built during the early days of the canal's construction. The only addition in all that time was an icemaker and refrigeration for the beer.

A haggard-looking older woman stuffed in a tight dress and wearing too much makeup and lipstick tossed Sam a bored look as he made his way to the bar. He gave her a shake of his head as he passed by and she went back to studying the contents of the glass she held in both hands atop the table where she sat.

At the bar, Sam put his foot on the edge of the porcelain trough running the length of the base of the bar that served as both footrest and urinal. He pushed a quarter across the top of the bar and ordered a beer.

"Una Nacional. Bien fria," he told the bartender, who looked more Arab than Panamanian. All Middle Easterners were called "Turcos" in this part of the world, but Sam thought that he was probably Armenian or Lebanese. The man fished a tall green bottle from an ice-filled cooler, deftly popped the cap off, held up an empty glass, and raised an eyebrow.

Sam shook his head and said, "Sin vaso." He wasn't about to drink from a glass in a place like this. The bartender put the glass back with the others on the bar and slid Sam the beer. He then walked to the far end of the bar, where he leaned on an elbow and put his face on the back of his hand and his ear next to a radio that was softly playing a Cuban bolero.

Sam worked the palm of his hand over the mouth of the beer bottle, lifted it to his lips, and turned to survey the room. The place was long and narrow, built like a shotgun shack in the American South. You could fire a double-barreled shotgun from the front door and hit everybody inside. At the back was a door set close to the right-hand wall. It led, Sam was sure, to the storeroom in back, which would have another door that led into the alleyway behind. In the bar itself there was no stairway to the floor above, but that didn't mean there wasn't one in the back room.

Sam took a short drink from the bottle, then set it on the bar and ambled past two stool-perched drunks to the corner where the bartender was cuddled up with the radio, listening with closed eyes. Sam rapped the bar with his knuckles to get the barman's attention and slid two dollars across the bar and under the man's nose. The bartender opened his red-rimmed eyes. He looked first at Sam and then at the money. He sat up, put out a hand, and covered the bills before giving Sam a vacant stare.

Sam pointed with his cane to the back room and asked about the stairway to the second floor he suspected was in there. "En el cuarto atras, hay escalera pa' arriba?"

The man lifted his hand from the money on the bar and spread the two bills slightly apart. He looked up from the money with a smirk and said, "Quien sabe."

Sam slanted his eye to the room in question. The bartender followed suit. When he did, Sam lifted his cane in a movement so smooth it appeared to be in slow motion but in reality was so quick it was impossible to deflect or deter. He jabbed the tip of the cane under the man's larynx and gave it a vigorous shove.

The bartender's head snapped backward and he was pinned against the wall behind. He felt excruciating pain in his throat. His vision blurred. He was choking, unable to breathe, but he didn't know why. He reached a hand to his throat, felt the stick, and through his tears saw Sam leaning across the bar, the stick between them. Sam released the pressure on the man's throat just a fraction and asked again, "Listen to me, hombre. Are there stairs back there?"

The bartender grasped the stick at his throat and tried to push it aside. It was a futile move. Sam punched the tip of the stick forward no more than half an inch, but it was enough. The man felt his throat close off. His sight went black, his hand fell away, and he dropped to the floor.

Sam looked over the bar where the man lay curled on the floor in a fetal position; gagging, coughing, and trying desperately to draw a full breath. He knew the bartender would be there awhile, his full attention given to his breathing difficulties, so he stepped around the end of the bar and opened the door to the supply room. Indeed, inside there was a door leading to the alleyway and a stairway that led to the floor above.

Sam stepped to the alley door and checked to see that it was locked. He then made his way to the top of the stairs and checked the door there. It was closed by a huge and ornately made padlock, so rusty it didn't look like it had been opened since Teddy Roosevelt was president. Sam doubted if a key for the thing still existed. The bartender could have easily saved himself some grief.

As Sam passed back through the bar he checked on the condition of the bartender, who had just gotten to his knees. He was head down, massaging his throat, and breathing in ragged, painful gasps. Sam put a ten-dollar bill on the bar and headed for the door. As he passed the two drunks seated at the bar, he saw one of them eye the bartender's money greedily and start to get up. Without stopping as he went by, Sam pushed the man back down on his stool and said, "Ni lo pienses, hombre"—don't even think about it.

The old hooker near the door gave Sam a wide, lipsticked smile as he passed. Sam lifted his cane in salute. When he had gone, she padded to the end of the bar, leaned over, and saw that the bartender was still kneeling on the floor gasping like a beached mullet. Acting quickly, she plucked his bills from the bar, tucked them into the top of her dress, and beat a hasty retreat.

The drunk Sam had warned away gave her a jealous look. Seizing the moment, he reached over the bar and grabbed a bottle of rum. He poured himself a stiff drink and slugged it down. Realizing his luck wasn't likely to run this good again anytime soon, he tucked the bottle under his arm, put his head down like a man in a storm, and scurried for the door. The other patrons watched him go with determined disinterest.

* * * *

Sam stood on the sidewalk and looked up the shadowed tunnel of stairway that led to the Hotel Corinto. He squared his hat just above his eyebrows, tapped his cane twice on the pavement, and began to climb. The stairs brought him on to a small landing in front of an open double doorway. He stepped inside to what was more of a vestibule than a lobby. To the right was a dim, dingy corridor and to the left was a counter with a rack of keys on the wall behind it. A single, bare, twenty-watt bulb hanging above the desk threw feeble light on the scene.

From behind the counter, a spiral of tobacco smoke drifted serenely to the cobwebbed ceiling. Sam stepped in just as a hawk-faced leathery old man rose from his chair behind the counter. The man stood still. He had a paperback novel in his hand. Smoke curled from a hand-rolled cigarette stuck in the corner of his mouth. He waited patiently for Sam to state his business.

It wasn't often that a man came to El Corinto alone, but it wasn't unheard of either. Occasionally a lone customer took a room and waited for someone else to join them. Usually that other someone was a woman, but sometimes it was another man—or a boy, or even a cueco, a man dressed and made up as a woman. Not that it made any difference to the desk clerk. He made no judgments as long as the patrons paid on arrival and kept their affairs quietly to themselves.

Sam looked closely at the clerk. He seemed familiar, and suddenly, seeing through the veil of intervening years, he realized he knew him. Ramon Dos Años was an old reliquiero—one of the handful of relic hunters who prowled the jungles and the mountains of Panamá in search of pre-Colombian artifacts to sell to collectors in the Canal Zone and in the city of Panamá. The man knew the interior of the country like his own front yard. Sam's father had hired him as a guide a number of times on specimen-hunting trips for the Smithsonian. Sam had considered him in those years as the most competent explorer and jungle expert he had ever met.

But he didn't let on now that he knew Dos Años. He didn't want to embarrass the man by acknowledging that someone he had known as a boy, someone he had looked up to, was now working the front desk of a whorehouse.

Sam knew that Dos Años was fluent in English—it was a requirement for cathouse desk clerks—so he addressed him now in that language as he took out a ten-dollar bill and placed it on the counter. "What can you tell me about the gringo in room thirty-four?"

Dos Años looked from Sam's face to the money on the counter and then back to Sam's face again. Sam pushed the bill across the counter so that it was closer to his hand. Dos Años didn't reach out to take the bill. He let it lay there and continued to study Sam's face.

After a bit, Dos Años took the cigarette from his mouth and said, "It pained me greatly when I heard of the passing of your father, Samuel. He was a good man. He was always fair with me, and he was always generous in his dealings with the Indians and the campesinos."

Sam reached out his hand. "Thank you, Don Ramon. My father thought a lot of you." They shook hands.

"And I've heard of you over the years"—Dos Años waved a hand vaguely toward the outside—"since the war, from some of the people who have dealt with you. They say you, too, are a fair-minded man."

Ramon Dos Años slid the money back across the counter. "So tell me, Samuel, what can I do for you? What is it you want to know?"

"Who is the man in room thirty-four?" Sam asked.

"A gringo, as you first said," Dos Años replied.

"Alone?"

Dos Años nodded. "Yes, alone."

"When did he check in?"

"Yesterday. The afternoon. About three, I think. Yes, three, I'm sure. He paid for four days in advance. That's very unusual."

"Any visitors? Maybe a woman?"

Dos Años shook his head. "Not that I have seen. And I'm here until midnight."

"Is he here now?" Sam asked.

Dos Años nodded and glanced at his watch. "He came in about forty-five minutes ago. He hasn't come back out."

"Describe him for me."

"Gringo. Thin. Dark hair. Pale skin. Young—he has maybe twenty-four, twenty-five years. Educated. He seems embarrassed to be here."

"Who else is in the place? How many other people?"

"Two couples. Just this floor."

Sam nodded to the key rack. "I need to check the room. Is there another key?"

When Dos Años turned from the rack and handed him the key, Sam picked up the ten-dollar bill and put it in the man's hand. The clerk tried to give the money back. Sam gently but firmly closed his gnarled fingers around the bill and made him take it. "It's yours, Don Ramon. No protests, please. And while I'm upstairs don't let anyone else past the desk until I return."

Ramon Dos Años reached under the desk and laid a long, keen-edged machete atop the counter. With a crooked smile he said, "No one gets by me until you say so, Samuel."

Sam bounced the key in his hand, nodded, and turned for the stairs that led to the next floor. On the third floor he came out into a dingy red corridor that smelled of disinfectant, stale smoke, rancid bodies, and sex.

He let his cane hang from its lanyard around his left wrist and held the key in his left hand. Reaching across his waist, he drew the Czech auto and slipped off the safety. Placing one foot directly and carefully in front of the other, and putting the entire sole of his foot on the floor with each step, Sam glided rapidly yet silently to the door of room thirty-four.

He paused at the edge of the door on the side nearest the door handle. Holding the key in readiness and the pistol at a slight angle away from his body, he stood utterly still and listened intently. The only sounds that came to him were the muffled noises from the street outside and a faint, rhythmic, bump-bump-bumping from the floor below.

Sam put the key in the lock and turned. The door wasn't locked. He gave it a push, let it swing open, and lifted his pistol. No sound of surprise came from the room. No one spoke from inside. Sam checked all he could see from where he stood by the edge of the door. He took two steps back to the other side of the corridor. His arm straight, he held his pistol in front of his face and stepped sideways, one quick step at a time, as he checked the rest of the room. No one home. He slipped the key into his pocket, lowered his pistol, entered the room, and closed the door.

The place was a wreck.

The narrow bed, an old GI cot, was tossed onto its side. What was left of the thin mattress was on the floor at Sam's feet. It was ripped to shreds, all the cotton stuffing spilled out across the floor. But it was the smell that told Sam what was in here. The rank, coppery, metallic odor was so heavy Sam could taste it in the back of his throat. A smell and taste he had experienced many times and meant only one thing.

Sam took another step into the room and saw the body. In reality, he first saw the great pool of blood puddled up in the far corner, carried there by the tilt of the uneven floor. The blood led back to the naked body of a man lying facedown on the floor just behind the bed. As he took a step closer, he realized that "facedown" was not quite accurate.

Rather, the corpse lay with its front side to the floor. The body could not be said to be facedown. That would have called for a face, and that was impossible. The dead man on the floor was lacking not just a face, but also a head.

Sam let his mind and senses roam the room in a series of overlapping mental snapshots. The place was a ten by twelve. No closet. The only furniture was the ruined bed, a small night table with the drawer flung on the floor, a rickety wooden chair with the seat ripped off and hurled aside, and a bare, dust-covered light bulb hanging by a frayed wire from the ceiling. The small lake of blood had not yet begun to turn brown, and Sam wasn't surprised when he knelt and placed his hand on the man's leg to find some warmth still there.

Sam studied the body. The man was white—probably American—and relatively young. He was medium size with an average physique—not muscular but not flabby either. His skin was pale and now ashen with death. The hair on his arms and legs was dark and thick. The body lay straight on the floor with the arms lying closely alongside the torso. The wrists ended in bloody stumps where the hands had been hacked off; the ends of the white bones gleaming obscenely. A puncture wound, maybe an inch wide, just to the left of the spine and slightly below the shoulder blade had wept a thin trickle of blood.

Sam stood and he felt the gore rise suddenly in his throat. He swallowed twice and gained control of himself. He stepped back from the body and stood stock-still. He took several long, deep breaths and gave the room another visual search. Not for what was there, but for what wasn't.

There was no suitcase, no overnight bag or even a shaving kit in the room. There were no clothes, no shoes. The sheets were missing from the bed, as was the pillowcase from the slashed and shredded pillow.

Sam stepped to the drawer of the nightstand where it lay upside down on the floor and turned it over with the tip of his cane. Underneath he found a pad of paper, a few envelopes, and the stub of a pencil. He picked up a sheet of paper, the pencil, and one of the envelopes and tucked them in the pocket of his jacket.

The stationary seemed to be the same as the note he had received that morning.

Standing again, he gave the room one last look, then stepped out and locked the door. He went to the far end of the hallway at the back of the building and looked out the open window. Cholo was in the alleyway and looked up immediately when Sam appeared in the window. Sam signaled for Cholo to come meet him at the hotel desk.

Sam put a hand in his pocket to make sure he had some change and then went back downstairs to use the pay phone he had seen on the wall in the vestibule. He breathed deeply and slowly as he went down the stairs. He had no difficulty admitting to himself that the discovery of the naked, decapitated body in room thirty-four of the Hotel Corinto had rattled him.

It rattled him because he knew deep down in his bones that such a violent death was meant as a message. But a message to whom, and from whom? And most importantly of all—what was the message?

NUEVE

Cholo was posted at the door of the crime scene. Sam had called Marta to arrange to have Walter Driscoll brought from Contadora back to the city. Sam personally called Major Jesús Rivera, chief of La Guardia's intelligence section, and asked him to meet at the El Corinto as soon as possible.

Sam and Rivera had an old, if not always smooth, professional relationship. Their main source of friction was almost always when American interests rubbed up against Panamanian sovereignty and each man had to back the position of his tribe. But Rivera knew that whatever this meeting was about, it had to be important for Sam. Sam didn't make direct requests such as this often.

Next Sam called Gorgas Hospital in the Canal Zone and arranged for an ambulance to be sent quietly to El Corinto to pick up the body of an American. Sam had no definite idea yet who the dead man was—at least, he wasn't sure—but he was almost positive that he was an American. He was also sure Rivera would object to the body being transported to the Canal Zone, so he wanted to get a leg up on the matter and let the force of inertia lend a hand.

Ramon Dos Años had watched quietly from behind his counter and had asked Sam no questions. It was patently obvious to him that something unusual had taken place. He waited patiently for Sam to address him.

Sam questioned Dos Años. "After the man in room thirty-four went up, did anyone else enter or come down?"

Dos Años noted the serious expression on Sam's face. He replied with a firm shake of the head and in a serious tone of voice. "No one, Samuel. Not a single person. Neither in nor out."

"And you, Don Ramon? Did you go up at any time?"

Dos Años shook his head again. "I have been here since I arrived this morning at seven."

"Have you left your desk at any time?"

"No. I take my meals here at the desk, and"—Dos Años indicated a partially open doorway behind the counter; inside the tiny room there was a sink and a toilet—"I piss with the door open so no one can sneak by me."

Sam smiled and asked, "Is there any other way into the building—from any of the floors?"

"No, Samuel. There was once an old stairway from the bar below, but it was nailed shut years ago."

"Show me, please," Sam asked.

The two men walked to the far end of the hallway and inspected the door in question. Not only was it nailed solidly shut, but the knob had also been removed. Even without the padlock on the other side, there was no access to be had through here. Sam walked the older man back to his station and told him some people, official people, would soon arrive. He gave instructions that they should be sent up to him on the third floor.

"And what is it, Samuel? What has happened? Can you tell me anything?" Dos Años asked.

"There is a dead body upstairs, Don Ramon. The guest in room thirty-four has checked out for good," Sam replied.

Ramon Dos Años considered a second before responding with a tight grin. "At least he paid in advance. When the people you have summoned arrive, I will send them up to you."

Sam nodded his thanks and went back upstairs to relieve Cholo of his vigil. He had shown Cholo the interior of the room before placing him on guard at the door. Sam had some ideas of his own but wanted to check them against the thoughts of his friend. He had great confidence in the opinion of his compañero.

"Don Ramon says no one entered or left after the man in the room came back this afternoon. So how did someone come in, kill him, and depart again with the victim's head, his hands, his clothes, and whatever belongings he had in the room?"

Cholo's dark eyes held Sam's steadily while he posed his questions. Then he turned and gestured Sam to follow. They went to the end of the hallway, to the open window, and looked outside.

Cholo pointed to an old iron pipe that ran up the side of the wall to the rooftop water tank. "Climb up to window. Kill the man. Put head in pillowcase. Roll clothes, shoes, everything up in sheet. Throw out window. Climb down. Go away. Not hard."

Sam let his eye roam up and down the deserted alleyway. He agreed this was how the killer had gotten in and out. As Cholo said, it wouldn't be that difficult for a man who was in any kind of shape.

"Do you think it possible anyone saw him coming or going?" Sam asked.

Cholo shrugged. "Maybe so. Want me to ask around?"

"Perhaps later. First I want you to go to Albrook Field and pick up Walter Driscoll. Bring him to the morgue at Gorgas. I'll be waiting there. You'd better hurry along. Major Rivera is on his way here."

Sam said that last part with a slight smile. Cholo Martinez and Major Jesús Rivera hated the very sight of each other. Sam had never been exactly sure what the source of bad blood between the two of them was, but whatever the reason for the grudge, they both clung to it fervently and nursed it with such tender care it made Sam think they both had an Irish branch in their family tree.

Cholo stared hard at Sam, turned on his heel, and left. Sam followed him to the other end of the hallway and watched him descend the stairs. Then he fished his Ronson and a cigar out of a jacket pocket and waited for Major Rivera to arrive. As he suspected, he didn't have long to wait.

Major Jesús Rivera was a tall, broad-shouldered, powerfully built man. His thick black hair was combed and pomaded straight back from a high forehead. He wore a mustache so narrow and precise it seemed to have been drawn with a pen. He looked out on the world with the dark gold eyes of a jungle cat. He was sleek, silent, and deadly—which is why friends and enemies alike knew him as El Tigre. As usual, he was dressed in mufti: a long-sleeved cotton guayabera, dark gabardine slacks, and the ubiquitous Panamá hat.

He and Sam had a bit of a go-round concerning where the body should be sent. Rivera had first insisted it should go to Santo Tomas Hospital and be kept in Panamanian custody while an investigation was conducted. But then Sam had politely pointed out to Rivera the responsibility he would have on his hands when word made it up channels that an American citizen had been decapitated in a Panamanian whorehouse.

One look at the savaged body was enough for Rivera to relent. Sam had asked him to come with him to Gorgas Hospital and that was where they were now, gathered around the sheet-covered body laid out on a stainless-steel table in the chill of the hospital morgue.

"What makes you so sure he's an American," Rivera asked in his deep bass-baritone voice.

"I'm *not* sure, Jesús. But I believe so." Sam threw back a corner of the sheet to reveal the man's leg. "That's the skin of a gringo."

Rivera studied the exposed leg, then glanced at his own bronze-colored hand and finally back to Sam. "There are white

Panamanians, Sam—the Rabi Blancos, the White Asses. They are whiter than you. You know that as well as I do."

Sam put the sheet back in place and patted the corpse on the leg. "Sure there are, Major. But I'll give you odds this man isn't one of them."

"But what if he isn't? What if he is Panamanian? What then?" Rivera asked as he reached up and tugged lightly on his earlobe, a sign Sam knew indicated that Rivera was already thinking three plays ahead of the game.

"In that case he reverts to Panamanian custody. No harm and no foul. And besides, it's not like he's going to get any more dead than he already is."

Rivera smiled. He'd let Sam take the lead in this, but he'd also make the most of the opportunity. It wasn't often that Rivera had a chance to gain some leverage over the gringos. His instinct told him that this was one of those rare occasions, and he was determined to make the most of it now. He fixed Sam with a stare that said *no negotiation.*

"I'll send a doctor, a *Panamanian* doctor, from Santo Tomas to conduct a joint autopsy. The body can stay in American custody until we are both agreed to its final disposition. My men will take charge of the murder investigation. I will share with you whatever we may find. I ask that you share whatever is pertinent under Panamanian law. If we apprehend a suspect, or suspects—of whatever nationality—and if the victim turns out to be an American, we will jointly determine how to proceed."

Sam held Rivera's stare. He asked with a thin smile, "Is that all, Jesús?"

Rivera replied with a smile that some people would have thought menacing. Sam, however, did not take it that way. "I think, Samuel, that is enough for a beginning."

"Then we are in accordance. Will you wait here for the autopsy?"

"I have other things of more pressing interest than staring at dead bodies. And I think I should make a preliminary report to my commander. I don't want him to hear of this from other sources."

"Oh, before you go, I have one last question."

Rivera arched an eyebrow. He felt an ambush coming on. He asked, warily, "A question?"

"Yes, a small one. Why are Villanueva's bodyguards following me?"

Rivera's eyebrows shot up in surprise. "Following you? Villanueva's bodyguards?"

"Yes, Jesús. Following me. Since they work for you, I thought you might know why."

Rivera paused and held Sam's look a bit before he spoke again. When he did it was in a flat, serious voice. "I don't know what you're talking about, Samuel. Even if it were so, those men don't work for me."

"Oh, it is so! And they do fall under your command, Jesús. The Guarda Espaldas of all Panamanian officials are assigned to La Guardia's intelligence service. Hence, you are their commander."

Rivera started to respond. He opened his mouth to speak. Then, thinking better of it, he said nothing. He stared, waiting for Sam to make further comment.

Sam obliged. "I didn't think they were necessarily following your orders, Jesús. If that had been the case I know you would have sent a better team; their tradecraft was pretty sloppy. But I did think you'd want to know that someone might be using your men for things you weren't aware of. Bad things have been known to happen when a man's subordinates have been co-opted by someone else. As goes an old saying, 'A man's enemies shall be they of his own household.'"

Rivera continued to hold Sam's gaze and remain silent. Sam could see the thoughts racing through the man's head. At last Rivera extended his hand. "You were right to tell me of this, Samuel."

Sam took Rivera's hand. "Hasta luego, mi Mayor. Vaya bien."

Rivera clasped Sam's hand firmly. "Cuidate, Sam."

Sam walked Major Rivera to the door to escort him out. Just as he reached out for the door, it swung open to reveal Cholo Martinez and Walter Driscoll. Rivera glanced at Driscoll and nodded his head. He looked coldly past Cholo and walked away without a further word.

Sam ushered the two men in and closed the door. He led them over to the body and threw back the sheet. Cholo leaned against a stainless-steel sink and began to clean his fingernails with the tip of his long switchblade knife. Driscoll stared down at the body.

Sam saw his Adam's apple bounce several times before he looked up at Sam with profound puzzlement in his eyes.

"Any of our people off the island and here in the city, Walt?" Sam asked in a neutral tone of voice.

Walter Driscoll swallowed again and nodded his head, not yet ready to speak. Driscoll wasn't a squeamish man, but the sight of the headless body had taken him aback. Walt was a good man, a decent man. And Sam knew that only a psychopath would be unmoved by the spectacle on the table. Sam gave the man a few seconds to allow him to regain his composure.

"Want to tell me who?" Sam asked.

"Two of the guards. Chambers and Moffitt."

"What are they doing here?"

"The members of the guard staff work a straight fourteen-day shift and then have a four-day furlough in the city. It was Moffitt and Chamber's turn for downtime."

"Do you know where they are, where they stay?"

"We keep rooms for the men at the Hotel Continental."

Sam knew the place. It was a good hotel that catered to upscale locals and foreign visitors.

"Are they there now?" Sam queried.

Driscoll looked worried. His eyes flitted from Sam to the corpse and back again. He hesitated before he answered. "I don't know, Sam. They were due back last night but neither of them has returned yet."

"Have you checked with the hotel?"

"Yes, Sam," Driscoll answered reluctantly. "Neither man checked in. They were never seen there."

"Is that unusual, Walt? For a couple of your guards to go AWOL and disappear like that?"

"It has happened before. Not often, but it has happened."

"And you didn't think it important to tell me?"

"Aw, Sam. I didn't want to bother you. You know how it is; the guys meet a couple of honeys and go off on a debauch. We're not talking about Boy Scouts here, Sam. These are some pretty rough men, but they always return."

"Until now."

"I'm hoping they'll turn up," Driscoll said meekly.

"How 'bout this one, Walt? What do you think? Do you recognize him? Is he one of ours?"

Driscoll looked the body over carefully before he spoke, and then it was in his professional voice. "The head and hands were removed to prevent, or to slow, identification."

"There was no clothing or personal belongings with the body either," Sam added.

Driscoll nodded. "Makes it even harder to determine an identity."

"So I ask you again, Walter—could this be one of our missing men?"

Driscoll continued to stare at the body. "I... I don't know, Sam."

"Chambers, as I recall, is a big man—a big, beefy red head. This couldn't possibly be him. Could this perhaps be Moffitt? What is Moffitt's first name?"

"Willis, Sam. His first name is Willis. And yes, the body shape and size and the tan on the arms are familiar. I've seen Moffitt on the beach. And another thing."

Driscoll stepped to the side of the body, looked closely at one shoulder, then crossed to the other side and looked at the other shoulder. He looked at Sam with a light of recognition in his eyes.

"This man's smallpox vaccination scar is on his right arm. So was Moffitt's. I remember seeing and remarking on it when we were playing volleyball one day. He said it was because he was left-handed and his mother had asked that the vaccination be done on that arm."

A vaccination scar on the wrong arm, thought Sam. *Yes, it could damn well be him lying here. But now the question is, where the hell is the other man, Chambers, and what has become of him? Is he also somewhere in the city, dead?*

"Walter, I think we have a problem. And I don't think we have any idea just how big it might be. I'm going to wait here for the autopsy. Cholo will take you to the office, and Marta will give you any help you need to see what information you can scare up on Chambers. What's his first name?"

"Alton. Alton Chambers."

"Alton Chambers. Okay. You begin your hunt with the Canal Zone authorities and I'll give his name and description to the Panamanians. Maybe we'll get lucky. Maybe, as you say, he's just laid up drunk with some little hootchie. Maybe, if we're real lucky, we won't find another body."

"Okay, Sam. I'm on it."

Driscoll turned for the door. Sam had a last thought.

"I forgot to ask, Walt. How are things on the island?"

Driscoll paused and said, "Tense, Sam. My team has carried on with the standard interrogations, and we're getting some good results. But Gottlieb and his assistants are still furious. Gottlieb makes it no secret that he views you as his main enemy. He'll poison you at headquarters if he can, Sam. He always brags that he has some solid supporters there. He also says he's sure your order will be rescinded. That's the only reason he's staying on."

"Well, if I can stay out of Dr. Gottlieb's professional clutches I think I'll manage all right," Sam said with a humorless smile.

"Yeah, if," Driscoll replied and then turned for the door.

Sam stayed on at the morgue until the conclusion of the autopsy. Both the pathologists—American and Panamanian—had reached the same determination. Cause of death was due to a stab wound to the heart rendered from behind. It appeared the knife used had a long blade and more than likely a double edge. Once inside the chest wall, the blade of the knife had been wrenched violently side to side; severing the top of the heart almost completely, lacerating both lungs, and leaving cut marks on the sternum and the front ribs. It was only then, after death, that the head and hands had been removed.

It takes a professional to kill like that, Sam thought. *Someone who knew what they were doing, was able to get within hand's reach of the victim, and then attack with cold-blooded ferocity. Someone who could look at another human being as only a target and kill without passion. Someone who had done this kind of thing before. Someone who relishes the act of intimate murder.*

Sam pictured the attack in his mind: The killer claps a hand over the victim's mouth and yanks his head back, rocking him up on his heels, throwing him off balance and unable to respond. At the same instant, he slams the knife in all the way to the hilt. Then he yanks the haft violently back and forth to inflict maximum damage. Most likely it had been done so fast the victim never knew what was happening. And more than likely he had felt no real pain—only a firm punch to the back and a slight sting when the knife was plunged in.

But who did this? Sam wondered. *Who and why? Why here, and why now? This sort of thing didn't happen out of the clear blue sky. There had to have been a cause a priori, hidden though it may appear now.*

And Sam knew, deep down inside, without the least shred of evidence yet to tell him so, that this was connected somehow to the operation on Contadora.

When Sam arrived back at his office, Marta told him that Walter Driscoll had sent a message to Agency headquarters asking for the personnel folders of Chambers and Moffitt and had then gone to Balboa to confer with the head of the Canal Zone Police. Cholo had left word that he was out on an errand.

Sam asked Marta to bring her steno pad and join him in his office. Once they were both seated, Sam dictated his report of everything concerned with the finding of the body and his suppositions surrounding the matter. Marta took the dictation down in swift shorthand and made no commentary. Even when Sam paused several times in order to gather his thoughts, she neither spoke nor looked up from her work. It was only when Sam finished with his dictation that she gave him a questioning look.

Sam returned the look and said, "Yes, Marta?"

Marta looked down at her pad as though seeking answers there before looking Sam in the eye and saying in a small, still voice, "Samuel, I think whatever this is about, it is aimed directly at you."

Sam held Marta's eyes for a few moments. "Once you've typed that report I'd like you to send a coded copy, Eyes Only, to Carleton Broadstreet at headquarters, make a copy for me, and lock the original in the safe.

"Then I'd like you to take some time off," he continued. "Perhaps a few weeks. Why not visit your sister and her family in Bocas del Toro? I know you haven't seen them in quite a while."

Bocas del Toro was a town on the Caribbean side of Panamá very near the border with Costa Rica. An old banana port, it was situated on an island at the mouth of a huge estuary. Bocas Town was about as remote a spot as could be imagined and still be called a place of civilization. The only access was by water or the occasional puddle-jumper plane. Sam was sure Marta would be safe there. Her sister was married to La Guardia's chief of police for the district, and any stranger arriving on the island, nosing around and asking questions, would stick out like a sore thumb.

Marta Fonseca studied Sam with solemn brown eyes before replying, "If you have no objections, Samuel, I'll take the early morning boat from Colón." She glanced at her watch. "Perhaps when Cholo returns he can take me home to collect some things and then drive me to the train station. If you need me before morning, I'll be in our rooms at the Washington."

Sam kept a suite of rooms at the Hotel Washington for use when he, or anyone else, needed to overnight or was working on the Caribbean side of the isthmus.

"That sounds fine to me. If Cholo's not back within the half hour I'll drive you myself."

Marta rose; Sam also stood. "Good," she said. "I'll get this typed and sent out. It will only take a few minutes."

Marta left the room and returned to her desk. Sam soon heard the typewriter briskly ratcheted as paper was inserted, and then the rapid-fire clatter of keys as Marta transcribed her shorthand text into a typed document.

Cholo returned and reported to Sam. "I ask on street, in alley, up and down block. Two people see gringo leave Corinto in afternoon. One saw him go back later, same as Dos Años say. Shoeshine boy see maybe same gringo on phone at Parque Santa Ana. Nobody see nobody in alley, climbing up or down, coming or going. But nobody always in alley. You want me keep asking?"

"Maybe later. First, send a boy to tell Don Julio I'd like to see him as soon as he can get here. Then, when Marta's ready, I'd like you to take her home to get some things and then to the train station. Go with her on the train to Colón and in the morning, see her safely on the boat to Bocas. After that, you can return here. De 'cuerdo?"

"Why I don't drive her to Colón? Is faster," Cholo replied, just as the typewriter fell silent in the other room.

"I don't want you on the Trans-Isthmian Highway after dark; it's just too dangerous."

"I drive good," Cholo responded, affront on his scar-crossed face.

"I know you do, hermano. It's the other things on the road I worry about: ox carts with no lights, campesinos drying coffee beans on the edge of the pavement, broken-down cars, kids playing, borrachos wandering down the center of the road. I know you can handle those things, but I don't want to put Marta's safety at risk."

"Ya caigo," Cholo replied with what for him passed as a grin. He was happy to know his driving skills weren't in question. Sam knew his right-hand man would do anything in his power to keep Marta safe.

Cholo touched a finger to his forehead and went out. Sam heard the outer door open and close as he went. In a few minutes Marta's sharp heels tapped across the room, followed by the sound of the Teletype machine in its closet, chattering away in raucous, staccato bursts. Then the machine went quiet. A minute later Marta entered and placed a thin manila folder on Sam's desk. She surprised him by coming around the desk and planting a kiss on his cheek before turning and leaving without a further word.

Soon Cholo returned and ushered the old street vendor into Sam's office. Sam could see Marta through the door. She had put on her hat and gloves and had her purse on her wrist. She glanced quickly at Sam and then turned away. Sam looked to Cholo, nodded his head toward Marta, pointed in that direction, and waved them away. Cholo nodded back, then turned and escorted Marta out the door. Sam felt older watching them go.

He turned his attention to his guest, Don Julio, the little fruit vendor who was the Cacique—the Chief—of Sam's legion of street spies. Over cigars and shots of bourbon, the two men generated a plan for Don Julio's watchers to keep a close eye on the surrounding neighborhood and to let Sam know immediately if anyone was seen taking too close an interest in the doings in and around Sam's office. He also asked that they keep an eye out for a new, green Hudson automobile and to scour the bars, bordellos, and hotels of the city—cheap and otherwise—for a big redheaded gringo named Alton Chambers.

Sam gave his friend sufficient money to pay for twenty-four-hour coverage, and enough also to spread around among the irregulars in the area. At the conclusion of their meeting, Sam knew for a certainty that a pissant couldn't cross the streets of Panamá City without it being seen and reported to him.

Sam escorted Don Julio to the door then returned to his office. He turned on the radio and listened to the evening news broadcast on the Armed Forces Network from Fort Clayton. Not long afterward, Walter Driscoll entered the office and dropped wearily into a chair. Sam turned off the radio and pointed to the bottle of bourbon still on his desk. Driscoll nodded yes. Sam grabbed a clean glass from atop the radio cabinet and began to pour. When the glass was half filled, Driscoll held up his hand to stop. Sam pushed the glass across the desk and refilled his own. The two men sipped their drinks in silence.

After a bit Sam lowered his glass and balanced it lightly on his knee. He looked at Driscoll and asked, "Learn anything worthwhile?"

Driscoll took another sip before placing his glass on the desk and replying, "The cop on duty at the ferry landing in Balboa remembered seeing Moffitt and Chambers when they came ashore, but he doesn't recall if they left the docks together or separately."

"Did he remember what they were wearing and if they had bags with them?"

"He did notice that. He said they were still in their khaki uniforms and that each man had an AWOL bag. Another Canal Zone cop who was on duty out on the street recalls seeing Chambers get into a taxi alone. He says he remembers him distinctly because he shoved a soldier out of the way and took the taxi. But he doesn't remember seeing Moffitt at all."

"I seem to recall that Chambers had been in the Marines. But what about Moffitt—he didn't appear to be a military type to me."

"All the guards have a military background of some type, Sam. I believe Moffitt had been in the navy but I don't know what his specialty was. When their records arrive from headquarters, we'll have a better idea of their histories."

"No matter what, we're going to need some replacement guards," Sam remarked. "Why don't I hire a couple of men here in the Zone? I think I can find us some reliable ex-soldiers."

"That would help matters for sure, Sam. We were already shorthanded, even before this."

"I'll get on it first thing in the morning. I'd like you to stay here for at least another day, if not two, and help La Guardia with the investigation. They could use your expertise. And I'll try to send the replacement guards out with you when you return, if not before."

"A day or two, sure. I can manage that. But I don't like being away from the island for very long at a time, Sam. I don't know what Gottlieb and his Prussian acolytes are liable to get up to in my absence."

Sam lifted his glass and smiled a tight-lipped smile. "We are entirely agreed on that point." He took a short sip of bourbon and continued. "We've been moving so fast since you got here that I've forgotten to inquire: did Marta get you situated for the evening? Do you have a place to stay?"

"She did, thanks, Sam. I've a room reserved at the Bachelor Officers' Quarters on Albrook, and I've drawn a sedan from the motor pool. In fact, I think I'll head on over to the BOQ now and check in. That is, if we have nothing more to do right now."

Sam stood. "No, go ahead, Walt."

Driscoll stood, hat in hand, and asked, "Why not join me for dinner at the Officers' Club, Sam?"

"Thanks for the offer, but I'm going to wait here awhile longer. I have a few calls to make yet. Anything turns up before now and the morning, I'll get you on the horn."

"Sure, Sam. Then I'll see you in the morning," Driscoll replied, and then turned to leave. He had taken only a few steps when he turned again and looked at Sam. "Do you think this was anything more than just a crazy killing, Sam? Do you think the project is in jeopardy? That other lives are at risk?"

Sam hesitated a heartbeat before saying, "I think something stinks in Panamá, Walter. But I'll be damned if I can figure out what it is."

Driscoll turned his hat in his hands, unconsciously working his fingers around the brim. "You'll let me know when you figure it out?" He asked the question with a humorless grin that was more of a grimace.

"Me, figure it out? Walter, you're the ace investigator here. I was counting on you to tell me," Sam rejoined.

Driscoll put his hat on and tugged the brim down over his right eye. "Well, hopefully we'll know more tomorrow than we do right now."

"There is always that hope, Walter. There is always that hope."

"Buenas noches, Sam."

"Hasta mañana, Walter."

With that, Walter Driscoll turned and left the office. Sam went back to his desk and read the transcript of his report. When finished, he put the folder in his safe and then went to the Teletype closet to check on any papers still there. He should have known that Marta had already disposed of the contents of the burn bag and locked away all other material before she had gone out.

Sam was back at his desk, the receiver of the phone in hand, finger in the dial, when the buzzer sounded at the front door. At first he thought it must be Cholo returning, but he realized Cholo should have been on the train with Marta by then.

Sam put the receiver back on the phone cradle. It had been a strange day, a crazy day, a day of unexpected events, so as a precaution he retrieved the Czech auto from his desk and held it handily at his side as he went to the door. He checked the fish-eye lens in the door and put his pistol away before opening up.

"Señor Ministro, this is a surprise. Come in, please." Sam pointed his chin in the direction of the two bodyguards standing just outside the portal. "And your men, they may come in also if it makes you feel more comfortable."

Jorge Villanueva gave Sam a sharp look before turning to his men and telling them to wait in the car. "Esperame en el auto."

The more senior agent glanced first at Sam, then back to his boss. He began to remonstrate, "Pero Señor—"

"Espereme afuera!" Villanueva barked.

The guard stepped back as though slapped. Sam gave them a shrug and a grin as he ushered the foreign minister inside and closed the door.

"Please, come to my office. May I get you a drink?" Sam asked as he led the way inside. He seated his visitor and then pulled his chair around from behind the desk so that they faced one another. Sam retrieved a fresh glass for his guest and, without asking again, poured a stiff whiskey. Villanueva nodded his thanks and took a sip as he looked around the room. Sam took a sip of his own and waited for the foreign minister to open the bidding.

Villanueva took another taste of the whiskey and put the glass on the desk. "You buy good liquor these days, Sam; not like that piss you used to drink."

Sam smiled as he took a pair of Macanudos from the box on his desk. He clipped the ends and passed one to Villanueva, who accepted with a nod of thanks. Sam said as he gave his visitor a light, "Uncle Sam pays for this stuff, Jorge. When it's on my dime I still buy the cheap stuff."

Sam lit his own cigar. The two men puffed slowly and studied each other through the blue screen of smoke. Sam Spears and Jorge Villanueva had known one another for most of their lives. They had attended the national university together. They had played sports together, argued politics together, chased girls and caught girls together. They had both seriously courted the same young lady. It was Jorge, however, who had won out and married her while Sam was away during the war. But for the last year or so the relationship had rekindled, and Sam had been sleeping with her now and then. But recently, with a mounting frequency, there was more now than then.

Sam wondered sometimes what, or how much, Jorge knew about his wife and Sam. And if, or when he found out, what he would do about it. For a man of Villanueva's position, family, standing, and status, it was one thing to admit that he was a cuckold, and another thing altogether to acknowledge it in a manner that was sure to become an article of public gossip and social ridicule.

Sam saw no reason to hurry matters along. So he sipped, smoked, and waited for Villanueva to state his reason for dropping in unannounced.

At last the foreign minister spoke. "Sam, I have come in person because I did not wish to make a phone call. I come on a matter of important business."

Sam studied the tip of his cigar and asked politely, "Is this, Jorge, a matter of public business or private business?"

Villanueva stared at Sam, his face an inscrutable mask. But Sam could see beneath the blank face, to that sharp mind working: weighing, sifting, selecting and discarding possible responses. It was not for nothing that Jorge Villanueva, young though he was, served as his nation's chief diplomat. A small country like Panamá could ill afford a political hack, or a moneyed buffoon, in such a delicate position. And in Jorge Villanueva, Panamá had neither.

The silence hung suspended in the air, where it drifted, swirled, and mingled with the delicate tendrils of cigar smoke. Villanueva looked off into nothingness. Sam looked at Villanueva. The seconds passed. Sam didn't mind the silence; he had the patience of a reptile. For him, patience was not just a virtue; sometimes, it was a weapon. So he smoked and waited.

At last Villanueva looked up and fixed Sam with his gaze. He asked, "Do you recall what Porfirio Díaz said about Mexico's relationship with its northern neighbor?"

Sam knocked the ash from his cigar before replying with a smile, "Don Porifio did have a way with words. He was supposed to have said, 'Ah, pobre Mexico. Tan lejos de Dios—tan cerca a los Estados Unidos.'" Poor Mexico. So far from God—so close to the United States.

Villanueva frowned and nodded. "At least Diaz never had to contend with a permanent Yanqui occupation right through the very heart of his country."

"Jorge, if this is the opening gambit for a renegotiation of the canal treaty, you're talking to the wrong man."

"No, Sam. I'm speaking about a different matter entirely. I'm speaking about a dead body—a murder—a murder committed on Panamanian soil. A most gruesome murder that may well be connected to your oh-so-quiet operation on Contadora. *That* is what I am speaking of, Señor Spears!"

"Ah, that," Sam replied softly, and took a pull on his cigar.

"Yes, that. You and your people have had a very free hand in Panamá, Sam. Whenever you've told us it had to do with the security of the canal we have said, 'Do as you will.' We have never liked it over much, but we have usually acquiesced. But now, with this murder, Sam, it is too much!"

"I don't know that the murder you speak of is connected to anything, Jorge. Neither I, nor Major Rivera, know for certain yet who the victim is."

Villanueva lowered the timbre of his voice. "But you are holding the body in American custody. You have taken possession, though the murder was committed on Panamanian territory."

Now it was Sam's turn to hold his silence. He studied the man across from him for several seconds before replying, also in a calm voice, "Tell me, Jorge. How go your negotiations with the

Russians over their request for a maritime bureau office? Have they come up yet with an acceptable...fee, shall we say?"

It was Villanueva's turn to smile. "Sam, my old friend, I thought you served the clandestine service? When did you switch over to the diplomatic side?"

Sam laughed aloud. He topped up Villanueva's glass, then his own. He took a sip and then said in a friendly tone, "Okay, Jorge. Out with it. You could care less about dead bodies and Contadora. What is it you want to tell me? Or want from me?"

As Sam spoke, Villanueva took a sip and then a pull on his cigar. "There are a few things, Sam. First, we *will* grant the Soviets a maritime office here in the city. As you suggest, it is now only a matter of price. And to keep you and your side happy, we will make no objections, say nothing, if you were to listen in on their communications."

"That's generous of you, Jorge. I'll pass that on to the interested parties."

"Please do. But of course, we expect to hear of anything that concerns us."

"Of course," Sam replied equitably.

"Secondly, I have quietly supported your efforts with the student union in the protests against Arosemena."

"*My* efforts?"

"Yes, Sam—your efforts. In fact, we are both using the same agents to destabilize the Arosemena administration."

"Oh Jorge, plotting against your own president! How could you?"

Villanueva ignored the jab. "We both desire the same result, Sam: Arosemena out of office. But, we want it accomplished without the possibility of bloodshed."

"Jorge, I've never—"

Villanueva held up his hand to cut Sam off. "I know what *your* sensibilities about these things are, Samuel. I am aware of your genuine affinity for Panamá. But I don't trust your people in Washington. I think there are some who would be very happy to see rioting in the streets or even an assassination. I think it would please them to have Panamá portrayed as just another unstable banana republic needing the firm hand and benevolent guidance of the North American Big Brother."

Sam took a puff and blew smoke toward the ceiling. "Then I take it there is a plan of succession in the offing?"

"More than just a plan. There is a compact, a political concordance."

"You have my interest, Jorge. Please go on."

Villanueva paused, considering just how much to divulge. In the end he decided to tell all, or almost all. "There will be no golpe de estado—no coup d'état—if that's what you are thinking. The protests—peaceful protests, mind you—will continue, and public support for Arosemena will continue to erode. In June, Colonel Remón will retire as chief of La Guardia and be asked to run for president as the candidate of the Liberal Party. He will dutifully accept the nomination, and he will be subsequently elected into office."

Sam blew a stream of smoke and grinned. "You seem pretty confident of that."

Villanueva furrowed his brows and answered, "No more so than in your own country. These things, as you know, are not left to chance; there is too much at stake."

"And you, Jorge? What is your part in the play?"

"I will become vice president under Remón."

"To keep the militarists at bay, is that it?"

"Even though Remón will be no longer in uniform, we know where his deeply rooted sensibilities lie. We cannot allow La Guardia to gain too much influence."

"A wise policy, I think. And a good choice for VP, I might add."

Sam lifted his glass in salute. Villanueva smiled and joined in. They each took a drink and then Sam asked, "Who will replace Colonel Remón as comandante en jefe?"

"Would you and your people object if it were to be your friend, Major Rivera?"

Sam smiled. "I think that is not only an inspired choice on your part but that it would also allay some concerns here on my side of the street."

"Then I take it you will pass this along, very quietly, to your superiors?" Villanueva asked.

"Oh, I have no superiors," Sam grinned. "You know my well-known pride and arrogance would never admit to that. But I will make sure that certain interested gentlemen in Washington are appraised of affairs."

Villanueva nodded. "Bueno! Then I take it we are in accordance: you will keep hands off this year's elections, and we will continue to ignore what takes place on Contadora. And when the Russians eventually have a maritime office here, we will both peel them like a fresh banana. Is that satisfactory to you, Samuel?"

Sam ran a few things through his mind, searching for trip wires, booby traps, and hidden minefields before replying. He was well aware of Jorge Villanueva's skill as a negotiator. But search as he did, he could find no hidden dangers. "Yes, Jorge. That is satisfactory. But I have one last question. What if Remón isn't content to wait? What if he were to seize the presidency before the elections take place? What then?"

"He wouldn't!" Villanueva spat.

"I've heard rumors to the contrary," Sam replied with an even expression.

"Then you've heard wrong!" Villanueva retorted.

Sam replied in a conversational tone, "Perhaps I have, Jorge. Politics is your area, not mine."

"I think you play games, Samuel, just to get a reaction," Villanueva pronounced.

"Oh well. Forget I ever said it," Sam rejoined in a cheerful voice.

Villanueva nodded his head and stood. He emptied his glass with a final gulp and placed it on the table. Next, with careful deliberation, he stubbed out his cigar in the ashtray. Now he looked Sam squarely in the eye.

"It was not by my orders that my guards were following you, Samuel. Nor were they operating under the orders of Major Rivera."

Sam also stood. He remained still and quiet and held Jorge's stare. Villanueva paused. He searched Sam's face as though fixing his features in his mind for all time.

"My wife..." He paused and cleared his throat. "My wife, Sam, is a woman of considerable passion. Sometimes, her enthusiasms lead her into excesses of emotional..." Villanueva faltered here, at a loss for words. Sam let him stumble.

"I know my wife, Sam. And I love her, even with—or despite...well, I hope—that is to say—I hope you will take that into consideration and exercise...exercise a sense of discretion and understanding."

Jorge Villanueva continued to stare at Sam. The look on his face not of pleading, but of a man asking another man for an honorable way out of a painful and embarrassing dilemma.

So he knows, Sam thought. *My God! What did it take for him to say those words?*

Sam let a friendly smile come into his eye. He extended his hand. "Jorge, I'm glad you came by this evening." The men shook hands. "And you have my word on everything we've spoken of, on everything that's transpired."

Sam walked Jorge to the door. When he reached for the door handle, Villanueva paused and looked at a spot on the floor. He pursed his lips, then nodded to himself before looking again at

Sam. "We must stay in closer touch, Samuel. Too much is at stake for either of us to jettison an old friendship."

"We are agreed there, also, Jorge. For many reasons, for every reason I can possibly think of."

Sam opened the door. The two bodyguards were waiting on the sidewalk in front of the building, standing together under the glare of the streetlamp. When they saw their boss in the doorway, the driver hurried to get behind the wheel while the other agent opened the back door of the car and stood by at attention.

Villanueva put on his hat. "Buenas noches, Samuel."

"Qué nos verémos muy pronto," Sam replied warmly.

Villanueva slowly descended the steps and got into the car. Sam watched the vehicle depart, then closed the door and returned to his office. He made a few other phone calls to set some things in motion for the next day. He propped his aching right leg on the desk, poured another drink, and pondered the events of the day.

He noted that during his conversation with Villanueva, neither of them had uttered the name Blanquita.

"Sufficient unto the day is the evil thereof," Sam said quietly to himself. Then he emptied his glass, turned out the lights, and locked up for the night.

DIEZ

The next morning Sam was up early. He received a call from Marta to let him know she was booked aboard the boat for Bocas and was about the leave the hotel for the docks. Sam asked her to send a telegram to let him know of her safe arrival. He then spoke with Cholo and asked that he stay with Marta until she was safely aboard, and watch until he saw the ship was past the breakwaters and at sea. Then he could return to the city.

Sam informed his elderly housekeeper, Gloria, there would be a guest joining him for breakfast and that she could serve them on the patio. He took a phone and plugged it into an outside jack so he could make some calls. Gloria brought him a pot of coffee and the morning papers and, a few minutes later, seemed a little disappointed when Walter Driscoll arrived for breakfast instead of one of Sam's lady friends.

Gloria poured coffee for Walter, served the food, and gave Sam a tight-lipped *humph* before going back to the kitchen. Once inside, she turned on the radio just loudly enough, Sam knew, to prevent the conversation outside from being overheard.

"Have a decent night, Walter?" Sam asked as he placed more pieces of bacon on Driscoll's plate.

Walter lowered his coffee cup and replied, "A quiet evening, Sam. Dinner at the club, a few drinks at the bar, then early to bed."

"Slept well, I hope?" Sam asked, before taking a bite of a thick corn tortilla.

"Not really. I woke up about three in the morning and couldn't get back to sleep. I kept running the situation over and over in my mind, trying to make sense of it. I'm sure that's Willis Moffitt's body lying in the morgue. But it makes no damn sense, Sam! It makes no sense at all!"

"It doesn't to us, Walt, not yet. But it does to someone. And I think we'll find out soon enough."

"Maybe, Sam. But I've investigated cases before that when you finally got to the bottom of them, and knew exactly what had happened, you still had no real idea of the *why*."

Sam nodded to acknowledge Driscoll's reasoning as he gave his attention to the meal. When finished, he pushed the empty plate away and refilled their coffee cups. Driscoll took a pack of Luckies from his pocket. He offered one to Sam, who declined, and then fumbled through his pockets looking for a match. Sam gave him a light from his ancient Ronson.

"I'd like you to man the office while I attend to some chores this morning, Walt. That is, if you don't mind."

"Glad to. One of us needs to be there in case the material on Chambers and Moffitt comes in. Can your equipment also receive photos?"

"Yes, if headquarters sends them, we can receive them."

"What about the body?" Driscoll asked. "If it proves to be Moffitt, what then?"

"I've asked Carleton Broadstreet to be prepared for that eventuality. If it is indeed our man, headquarters will notify the next of kin, and the body will be shipped to the States. A cover story will be concocted for the family. Something plausible and suitable, I'm sure."

"Yeah, I'm sure," said Driscoll said dryly, with a sad shake of the head.

"Back to the present problem, though. I mentioned that I'd like you to work with La Guardia on their end of the investigation. Not as a detective, but I would like you to touch bases with Major Rivera and provide him what assistance you can before you return to the island. I think it would go a long way to lessening any friction between our mutual services."

"I'd be glad to. At present it seems we're on hold anyway."

"Thanks. I spoke with Rivera last night and ran the idea past him. He was very receptive. I'll give him a call and let him know you're available to help out. By the way, I'd forgotten to ask; how's your Spanish?"

Driscoll held his out hand, palm up, and turned it side to side. "I speak it, but only so-so. And this Panamanian dialect gives me a lot of trouble. Most of the time, I don't have the slightest idea what's being said."

Sam smiled. "No worries, Walt. Rivera speaks English, and most of his investigators do as well. It's your presence that will mean the most to them. It indicates a certain level of trust."

Driscoll drained his cup, stubbed out his cigarette, and stood. "Then I'll get on with the day, Sam, and see what we can find."

Sam also stood. He reached into his pocket and handed Driscoll a set of keys. "Here, you'll need these. The big one is for the front door, the other is to the Teletype closet. If you need to send or receive any messages, the cipher pad is in the safe inside the radio cabinet in my office." Sam gave Driscoll the combination orally. Walt repeated it back with no difficulty.

"Okay, Sam. See you later?"

"I'll see you at the office later in the morning; before lunch I hope. Cholo should be back in an hour or so. When he arrives, ask him to wait until I return, please."

Driscoll pocketed the keys and put on his hat. "Okay, Sam. Hasta luego."

Driscoll departed. Sam poured another cup of coffee as Gloria cleared the table and then went back to the kitchen. Sam sipped his coffee and determined the order of business for the day. He picked up the phone and made the first of several calls. Then he took the phone back inside and retrieved his hat, cane, and jacket. On his way out he told Gloria he would not be returning until the evening. Then he got into his car and descended from his home on Quarry Heights for the short drive to Fort Clayton.

* * * *

Sam had alerted Captain Harris, the commander of Fort Clayton's MP company, the evening before about what he needed from him. He had known Harris only slightly and was surprised to find the man not only receptive but also helpful.

Harris was a very young-looking man with a bright, ruddy complexion, keen blue eyes, close-cropped sandy hair, and a very earnest and straightforward demeanor. But he was no kid; Harris had earned his captain's bars as a company commander in combat in Korea.

He looked at Sam across his desk and spoke as though making a report to his superior officer. "I've started Sergeant Turner's paperwork already, Major. He goes on temporary duty, assigned to you, effective as of today. His official retirement date will be at the end of the month. He can sell his unused leave back to the army at that time."

"I'd like for his family to stay in their on-post housing until I can make other arrangements—certainly no later than the end of the month. Would that be a problem, Captain?" Sam asked.

Harris smiled and shook his head. "None at all. If that's the least the army can do for Sergeant Turner after more than twenty years' service, I'm happy to make it happen."

Sam rose to leave. "Then I'll let him know he can take off the uniform—or would you rather do that?"

Captain Harris stood up. He chuckled and said, "Why don't you tell him? He'd like it better that way. To tell the truth, I don't think I rate too highly in Sergeant Turner's estimation."

It was Sam's turn to chuckle. "These crusty old NCOs can be a little hard to handle sometimes. They believe, and rightfully so in my estimation, that the army belongs to them. But Captain, I can assure you from personal experience that if he hasn't thrown you out a window yet, Turner thinks the world of you."

"Then I'll take that as a compliment and wish Sergeant Turner all the best in his new life as a civilian. You'll find him waiting for you in the first sergeant's office."

Captain Harris and Sam shook hands. "Thank you, Captain. I appreciate your help with this. I honestly don't know how you pushed this through so quickly."

"My pleasure, Major. Stay in touch."

Sam touched a finger to his forehead and went in search of ex-sergeant Nolan Turner.

* * * *

Sam and Turner walked together to the parking lot. They stood in the shade of a mango tree near where Sam's Ford was parked.

"Were you able to get in touch with Connor Sims?" Sam asked.

Sims was another old soldier who had served with Sam and Turner during the war. He, like Turner, had married a local girl and stayed on in Panamá after his discharge. Sam had used Sims before on a few occasions. The man wasn't the brightest star in the sky, but he was as brave as a Jesuit priest and as quiet as the grave—both positive attributes in Sam's book.

Turner nodded. "Yeah, he's ready to go whenever you say. Itching to go, as a matter of fact."

"Good. Here's what you'll be doing: I'm posting you as guards for a project on Contadora. Pack a bag with four sets of khakis—no insignia—boots, pith helmet, and a couple of sets of casual civvies. You'll be issued everything else you need once you get to the island. A man named Walter Driscoll is in charge out there. While on the island, you and Sims will take your orders from him. He'll brief you on your duties when you get there. But never forget, you're working for me."

Turner nodded his crew-cut head. "Got it, chief."

"But here's where things shift gears a bit, Nolan." Sam handed Turner a small cigar box. "Inside—no, don't open it here—is a snub-nosed .38. I want you to tape that to your ankle and keep it on you at all times. I hope you'll never need it, but I want it on you. Always. One man from the island has died and another has disappeared; those are the ones you and Sims are replacing. I don't want anything happening to either of you."

"No worries, Major. You know I can handle myself."

"I know that, Nolan. I just want you to be aware."

"I will, sir."

Sam continued: "Also in the box is a playing card: the jack of diamonds. On the day you arrive, I want you to give it to one of the detainees on the island, a man named Dimitri Demitrova. When you know you're unobserved, hand him the card and say, 'Sam sends.' Then walk away and have nothing else to do with him after that."

"Can do easy," Turner replied.

"After you've given the card to Demitrova, and when you're by yourself, I want you to peel back the paper cover from the top of the box. Inside you'll find instructions for you and you alone. When you've read them, burn the paper and scatter the ashes. No one, not even Sims, can know about any of this. You got me Nolan? It's that important."

Turner's face was a study in seriousness as he replied, "Yes, Major."

Sam looked at his old sergeant and said, "Nolan, things are not as they should be on the island. Something's screwy out there. I'm not sure exactly *what* is wrong but I feel that something is. You're going to be my eyes and ears on the island. And if things go south, I trust you to use your judgment."

"You can count on me, sir," Turner solemnly replied.

Sam smiled. "I know that, Nolan. And from now on, it's Sam. Not Major and not sir. Think you can do that?"

Turner smiled also. "May take a little getting used to, but sure, Sam. I think I can swing that."

Sam gave the big man a friendly pat on the arm. "Okay then. Go grab Sims and make ready. I may need you to fly out later today but more than likely it will be tomorrow. Any questions just now?"

"Just one...Sam. This man, Driscoll. You trust him?"

Sam hesitated before answering. "You know how sometimes you take a shirt out of the closet, and before putting it on you wonder if you've worn it before, if it's dirty or not?"

"Yeah, I've done that before."

"Well, I had that happen one day when I was still in school. And I asked the lady who kept house for us what she thought—was the shirt clean or not? Know what she said to me?"

Turner shook his head.

"She said, 'Sammy, if you have to ask...if you have even the least doubt, then the shirt is dirty.' Does that answer your question, Nolan?"

"Loud and clear, Sam. Loud and clear."

"Okay, my friend. Get yourself squared away and be ready for a call. Oh, and here...Sam handed Turner an envelope. "Split that with Sims. It's to take care of any expenses you may have getting ready. Just receipt me later."

Turner pocketed the envelope. "Wilco, Sam."

Sam got into his Ford and waited until Nolan Turner had driven away. When he was out of sight, Sam cranked the engine and headed in the opposite direction, back through the cantonment area of Fort Clayton to see Ilsa Matuzak about a nagging thought that had come to him during the night and would not let him go. If anyone would have the answer, he thought, it would be Ilsa.

* * * *

Sam parked on the mountaintop commo site and then made his way down to the dungeon, as he thought of it, where Ilsa and her ladies held quiet court. Ilsa greeted him with a surprised look on her face. Sam had never come unannounced before; she was worried his arrival brought bad news.

Ilsa took his hat and cane and led him to her table. Sam noticed the furtive glances from the women at their workstations around the room. They, too, were puzzled by Sam's unexpected arrival.

Sam spoke first. "Calm yourself, Ilsa. Nothing is wrong. I just have a question, that's all."

Sam noted the relief in her face at his words. He knew she had lived much of her life in places where surprises were seldom good.

"That is a relief, Samuel. Now, what can I do for you? How may I help?"

"What do you hear from the Russian trawler? When was its last transmission?"

She looked down at the tabletop for a second before she looked back up at him over the rim of her dark glasses. "That which you ask is something I, too, have been thinking about, Samuel. They have gone quiet—nothing since you were here last."

"So we have no way of knowing their location either, do we?"

"No, Samuel. I'm afraid we don't," she replied in a hollow voice.

Sam touched the corner of his eye patch. He then placed his hand on the table and drummed his fingers in three sequences of three taps each before speaking again. "Do you know the frequencies they used for transmission?"

"Yes, Samuel. We know the ones they had been using. They changed by the day of the week and by blocks of hours, but we figured out the pattern rather easily. However, as I said, they have been quiet."

"Quiet, yes. But if I had an agent in the field, no matter what, I would be listening. You know, just in case of an emergency. For what we used to call a 'report by exception.'"

Ilsa's face enlivened. "Yes, Samuel. Exactly so!"

"Then...what say we bump our comrades out there on the high seas? Let's shoot them a short message on the appropriate frequency and see if we can get them to come up for air. If they take the bait, then we'll have an angle on them; a heading to go by to help determine their location."

She was ahead of him. She was already up and striding to a radio console in the corner of the room. She looked behind her and motioned impatiently. "Come, Samuel. Come."

She sat down, put on a headset, and turned on the equipment. While it was warming up, she plugged in an old-fashioned Morse code key set. She looked over her shoulder at Sam as she lightly touched the set. "The Soviets still use the old equipment. I happen to favor it also. It is always reliable."

Ilsa checked the time by the large government-issue clock on the wall. She next consulted a logbook she had at hand and dialed in a frequency on the transmitter/receiver. She listened for a bit and carefully tuned several of the knobs. Finally, she glanced back at Sam and gave him a tight smile. "Something nonsensical, I think. How about, 'I have a lovely bunch of coconuts'?"

Sam laughed aloud. "Couldn't be better."

Ilsa smiled at Sam and then gave her full attention to the Morse set. She rested her finger lightly over the key and closed her eyes. She paused for a beat and then her hand danced rapidly on the enamel-topped lever beneath her fingertips. The burst was no more than three seconds. She waited for a count of five and tapped out the message again. Then she flipped a toggle switch on the radio, lifted her headset, and sat back in her chair.

She looked at Sam over her shoulder. "Now, we wait and see."

The radio hissed mindless white noise for several minutes. Just as Sam began to doubt if they'd been heard, the set chattered a brief reply. Ilsa looked at a dial on the face of the set and quickly wrote down some numbers. Then she tapped out the original message again. They waited another five minutes but there was no further response. Ilsa left the radio set turned on and stood.

"They took the bait. As you said, Samuel, they came up for air."

"What did they say?" Sam asked.

"'What,'" Ilsa answered.

"What did they say, Ilsa?" Sam asked, more urgently.

"What. Sam—they asked, '*What?*' Nothing more. I think the operator made an unauthorized response and was cut off by an adult in the room. I would imagine some poor comrade is being severely chastised as we speak."

"But was the transmission long enough to get a heading?" Sam asked, his excitement building.

Ilsa tore a page from the notebook. "Oh yes. All we needed was for them to break squelch." She handed Sam the sheet of paper. "Here, Samuel, the heading to their location at the time of transmission: one hundred twenty-seven degrees, magnetic."

Sam looked briefly at the sheet in his hand before he tucked it away in his jacket. His face lit up.

"Ilsa, my love! You're an absolute miracle worker! And we do a great Abbott and Costello together! What! Who said 'what'!"

Before she even knew what was happening, Sam took Ilsa by the shoulders, pulled her close, and gave her a big kiss. Though surprised, Ilsa didn't resist Sam's happy embrace. In fact, she folded into him and felt her breasts push against his broad chest. The other ladies in the room all glanced over, each with varying degrees of envy.

Sam released her and stepped back. She opened her eyes and stood still, clutching her arms awkwardly. She blinked several times; opened her mouth, and then closed it. She didn't know what to say. Fortunately, Sam did.

"Mind if I use the New Jersey phone?" he asked with a bright smile.

She nodded and pointed to the phone. Ilsa didn't trust herself to speak. *It has been a long time,* she thought. *A long time since a man has taken me in his arms.* She was surprised to find she missed it—the human contact. Sam's kiss had awakened something that had been lying dormant for much longer than she wished to think on.

Sam hurried over to the phone and dialed a number. He touched the edge of his eye patch and tapped a toe as the call went through and began to ring. Then a voice answered.

"Flight Ops, Lieutenant Gaddis speaking, sir."

"Eddy, how soon can you have the plane ready?" Sam asked, excitement in his voice.

"Soon as you can get here, sir," replied the flight lieutenant.

"Then kick the tires and light the fires; I'm on the way."

"I'll meet you on the apron, sir. Ready when you arrive," Gaddis laughed in response.

Sam hung up and turned around to find Ilsa Matuzak nearby, a hand on the locket of her necklace. Sam stepped close and took her other hand.

"Ilsa, I'm sorry to be so abrupt but I must leave. I owe you for this. You are a treasure. When this is over we must have dinner," he said in a rush of words.

He lifted her hand to his lips, suddenly faced it palm up and kissed it, and was gone before she could speak. When the door closed behind him, she returned to the room of bustling machines and women who listened to secrets every day. The listeners smiled at her wistfully and then directed their focus back to work.

Ilsa went back to her desk. She shook a cigarette from its pack and fitted it into her prized carved ivory holder from another time. She noticed her hand trembling as she brought the lighter to the tip of the cigarette. Ilsa Matuzak, veteran of many wars, smoked her cigarette and traced Sam's kiss in her palm and remembered that she was a woman.

ONCE

Sam adjusted his headset and keyed the hand mic for commo with Lieutenant Gaddis via intercom, next to him in the cockpit.

"Take us out over the mouth of the canal and then bring us on an easterly heading toward Isla Chepo. Let's hold an altitude of fifteen hundred feet," he said.

"Easterly to Chepo. Fifteen hundred," Gaddis replied.

Sam watched the scenery crawl by below as they climbed to altitude. The anchorage was surprisingly free of shipping; just a few freighters swinging on their chains and awaiting passage. He watched as a pilot boat hurried out to meet an incoming ship. Both vessels merged smoothly, neither slowing its speed. As soon as they came alongside, the Pan Canal pilot jumped aboard and on the bridge to guide the ship across the isthmus.

Just off the tip of the Fort Amador causeway and immediately past the joined islands of Naos and Perico, Gaddis turned to the new heading. They flew along parallel to the shoreline and to the city of Panamá. Sam loved this sight. The only thing prettier, he thought, came after spending days fishing offshore and heading back in. Seeing the city emerge from the surface of the sea then was almost a miracle.

Chepo was a small island twenty miles or so to the east of the city, at the mouth of Rio Chepo. There was a small fishing village on the island, but this was of no concern now; Sam was merely using the island as a landmark for the next leg of the flight. When they were over the island, he issued new instructions.

"Turn us south toward Isla Del Rey. Then run us down between the eastern side of the island and the mainland. Hold a course that would give us landfall at the village of Jaqué."

"South to Del Rey, on course to Jaqué," Gaddis repeated as he veered right onto the new heading.

Sam felt the plane slip sideways under the force of the trade winds that now took them full on the port side. Gaddis adjusted the tail trim to counteract the slip. Ahead some twenty-five miles out, the Pearl Islands came into full view. Contadora, the farthermost island on the northeast corner of the archipelago, was just a smear on the sea. Sam was certain that at this altitude and distance, as well as silhouetted against the mountains of the Darién, they were practically invisible to any possible lookout there.

The plane droned on and soon they were approaching the northern reaches of Del Rey, the largest island in the Perlas.

Gaddis keyed the mic to the intercom. "Will we be making a landing at Jaqué?"

Sam spoke into the mic, "Not sure yet. Just hold course and head in that direction. I'm looking for something to the south of Del Rey. Keep us on this side of the island, with the sun behind us."

"Roger," replied the lieutenant.

That's one of the things I like about Eddy Gaddis, Sam thought. *He doesn't ask a lot of unnecessary questions. Just what's pertinent for the task at hand.*

As the plane came even with the southern point of Del Rey, Sam saw a dark spot on the ocean. It was maybe ten miles or so away to the south. He lifted a pair of binoculars to his eye for a better view, adjusted the focus, and zoomed in. It was a ship.

Sam handed Gaddis the binos and took the yoke of the plane. "I've got her, Eddy. Here, your eyes are twice as good as mine. Take a look and tell me what you see."

Gaddis lifted the binos and scanned in the direction Sam had indicated.

"It's a ship, Major. She's making no wake, and her bows are pointed into the wind. I can't tell for sure, but it looks like she's anchored."

Gaddis handed Sam the binos and took back control of the plane. He keyed his mic again and asked, "Is that what we're looking for?"

"Maybe," Sam replied. "But I only want to make one pass. Crab us over so that it doesn't look like we're altering course, but bring us about a half mile off their starboard side for a better look. Then take us on in and land at Jaqué."

"Roger that."

Lieutenant Gaddis took some of the trim off the controls and let the trade winds drift the plane, ever so subtly, closer to the ship. He timed it so that they were within the half mile Sam had asked for just as they came abeam the vessel.

Sam held the binoculars steadily on the ship as they went past. She was a rust-covered old fishing trawler that looked like she had been at sea for ages. The bow markings were too grimy to make out a name, but as they went past the ship Sam turned in his seat for a look at the stern. It took a few seconds for him to make it out, but then he was sure.

SVETLANA, SEVASTOPOL, written in Cyrillic script, was visible in faded lettering just below the aft rail.

"How far off the island would you say she is, Eddy?" Sam asked.

Gaddis made a quick scan of his instruments. "She's eight... maybe ten miles out, nautical miles, that is."

Just outside Panamanian territorial waters, Sam thought. *And funny thing about that trawler. She had no booms or nets, but she does sport an awful lot of radio antennae from her superstructure.*

"Okay, Eddy, take us on in to Jaqué," Sam said, looking at his watch. "It's still lunchtime and I know a lady there that sets an excellent table under her bohio. She serves a superb sancocho with rice, and guandoo, and a big jar of chicha to drink."

"Sounds good, Major. Turning final for Jaqué," Gaddis responded. Within minutes he brought the plane to a gentle landing on a grass strip tucked into a fold in the Darién Mountains, just at the edge of the remote and lonely native village.

* * * *

"Take us back along the coast, Eddy. Keep your altitude no higher than one hundred feet until we get near the city," Sam instructed just after takeoff from the strip at Jaqué.

"Hugging the coastline, altitude one hundred feet," repeated Lieutenant Gaddis.

Sam looked back at the village after they had cleared the mouth of the river and were well clear of the shoulder of the mountains. He was glad this was dry season. He knew from experience about that landing strip: it was one helluva muddy place to land when the wet season was in full swing. He swiveled his head to look left, in the other direction. The Russian freighter was just a dark smudge on the brilliant blue surface of the Pacific.

The return flight was uneventful. Gaddis brought the plane in over the mouth of the canal and just past Sosa Hill, then made a hard right to bring them to final approach on Albrook Field. The headwind was so stiff this time of day that Sam was sure their ground speed was no more than thirty knots when Gaddis touched down on the tarmac. Within minutes they were parked on the apron.

Sam waited to take his leave until Gaddis had the plane tied down and the chocks were under the wheels.

"I know I don't have to remind you, Eddy, that today's flight was on the QT. Location—what we saw—all that sort of thing."

Gaddis took Sam's extended hand. "No, Major. That goes without saying. But you know what?" He lowered his voice conspiratorially. "I have way more fun flying these jaunts for you than if I were ferrying around the chief of staff of the army!"

"Okay, Eddy. I know I can depend on you. May need you to take some men out to the island tomorrow. Will you be available?"

Gaddis grinned again. "I sorta hinted something or other to the colonel recently—dropped your name kinda like—and you know what? Oddest thing happened. Seems I fly only for you now. That is, until, as the colonel said, 'you screw it up, Gaddis!'"

Sam laughed at the thought of Eddy working a hoodoo on his commander. "Okay, Eddy. I'm glad to have you with us full-time. I'll let you know later today, but plan on a flight in the morning. It'll be three pax and some baggage."

"You call, we haul, Major."

"Thanks, Eddy. I'll be in touch."

Sam unlocked his car and opened both the passenger and the driver's door to let the heat out of the vehicle. The dry season sun was beating down with pure ferocity, but the trade winds soon whipped the heat out of the car and he was able to get in. He'd recently read in *Life* magazine that Chrysler was offering air-conditioning on its premium vehicle line-up for the 1953 models.

Air-conditioning! Imagine driving a car in Panama with air-conditioning! Sam loved his Ford Coupe but this was too much. He wasn't wild about Chrysler. But he wasn't wild about driving with the windows rolled up during rainy season half the time. Or using the trade winds to beat the heat off his leather seats.

I think I'll have to look into buying a Chrysler, Sam thought. *I could pick out a car and have it shipped down on the Canal Zone barge from New Orleans. The new models come out in September. Yeah, that's what I think I'll do.*

Sam thought about what model car he might buy the whole time he wheeled out of Albrook Field, turned left, and cruised through the Canal Zone headquarters town of Balboa and was snagged by a light in the middle of town. When the light changed, he had just moved on to the issue of colors for the new car when he passed the YMCA building on his right and caught a glimpse of the green Hudson Hornet far back in the parking lot under a spreading rubber tree.

Sam was already past the last entrance into the YMCA parking lot. He glanced in his rearview to see if he could stop and do a U-turn, but a line of cars was behind him stacked up bumper to bumper at the light. Sam pushed the shifter up into second and slammed his foot down on the accelerator. The pair of two-barrel carburetors sucked air and gasoline and spit the volatile mixture down the intakes of the big V-8 flathead engine. The rear tires yelped and spit smoke and the Ford Coupe leaped forward as if shot from a cannon. He held his hand on the gearshift, holding it in second. Ahead, in the oncoming lane, he saw a break in the traffic—just a gap of about three car lengths—but it was enough.

As he came even with the next-to-last car in the other lane, he reached down and yanked the hand brake hard—as far back as it would go. The rear wheels locked up and screamed in protest, hissing out a cloud of stinking blue smoke.

As the tires began to slide on the pavement, Sam gave the wheel what looked like a lazy quarter turn to the left. The front wheels became the pivot point as the rear wheels came around, with the car sliding backward in the other lane and facing back in the other direction.

Traffic in both directions locked up as the startled drivers pounded on their horns. Sam released the hand brake and stomped the brake pedal to stop the momentum of the backward slide. He double-clutched, slammed the car down into first gear, and jumped on the accelerator again. The car leapt forward, back in the direction of the intersection. The entire maneuver had taken about three seconds and scared the daylights out of the nine drivers and four pedestrians who scrambled away from the action.

Sam hit the horn and made a sharp left turn, cutting across the lane in front of another startled driver, and whipped full speed into the YMCA parking lot. He flew to the lot on the other side of the building, where he found—nothing.

The Hudson wasn't there. Sam knew he had seen it. You can't confuse a rare Hudson Hornet for any other automobile. He tooled calmly around the parking lot, looking up and down the spaces. Still nothing. He drove to the front of the building and looked back and forth from the intersection.

The Hudson could have bolted in one of four ways. If it had gone back onto the main road and headed north, Sam was pretty sure he would have seen it; he had a straight view in that direction.

It hadn't pulled out to follow him as he went past—he was sure of that. That left two possibilities: a turn on Amador Avenue and into the maze of side streets in that direction, or a jump across the street and over behind the church to the neighborhood around La Boca. Sam ruled out La Boca because everything there dead-ended against Sosa Hill or bumped up against the bank of the canal.

Sam turned the Ford to the left and headed slowly in toward Amador Avenue. When he came in sight of the entrance gate to Fort Amador, he turned left again and began to cruise the streets of the neighborhood. He idled along, up one street and down the other, looking into carports and parking spots and behind buildings. Still nothing. It was as though the Hudson had vanished into oblivion.

Sam came back to Amador Avenue and turned to the right. As he approached the YMCA building again, he noticed an animated group of people standing in the parking lot talking to a Canal Zone cop in his cruiser. When he drove past, one man looked up, pointed excitedly at Sam, and yelled, "That's him! There's the maniac!"

A chorus of voices joined in, "Yeah, the crazy driver! That's him all right!"

Sam pulled to the curb and switched off the ignition. If this were just over the line in Panamá, Sam would have given the Guardia traffic cop two bucks and a cigar, and that would be that. But this was the Zone, where things went by the book, and the rules mattered.

Sam took the special ID he carried out of his wallet before getting out of his car and waiting for the cop—he didn't want the man to turn on his lights or siren and make this any more of a spectacle than it already was. It was just better this way.

Maybe a green car, he thought. *They disappear like magic.*

* * * *

Back at his office, Sam read the note from Driscoll saying that if needed, he could be reached via Major Rivera at La Guardia's intel HQ. It was obvious that Cholo had also been in; he'd left a note in Spanish saying he was out checking with Don Julio and would return in a while. Sam decided this was a good time to go over Driscoll's report of the situation on Contadora and listen to the tapes of the interrogations. He pulled the new tape machine from the Teletype closet and wheeled it into his office. This new device was much simpler and easier to set up than the old wire recorders he was accustomed to.

Sam had just begun to thread the first reel of tape through the machine when the phone rang. His first inclination was to let it ring, but then he thought it might be Driscoll or Cholo. So he picked up the receiver, leaned back in his chair, and answered, "Aqui habla Sam."

"Hullo? Hullo?" said a woman with a British accent in a slightly husky voice. "I'm calling for Mr. Sam Spears, please."

Sam smiled as he responded, "Lady Swathmore. What a lovely surprise!"

"Oh Sam. I'm so glad to have finally reached you. The phone system here is utterly wretched. I do hope this is not an inopportune moment?"

"Not at all, Felicity. I'm delighted to hear your voice. To what do I owe the honor?"

"Well, you *did* offer to show me some of the sights. I hope I'm not imposing, but I have the afternoon free, and if, well, I thought I would take you up on your gracious—"

Sam interrupted her, glancing at his watch at the same time. "Where may I pick you up, dear lady?"

"Oh, then you don't mind? That's ever so kind of you. Would it be convenient to meet me at the residence in, say, half an hour?"

"I'll be there in twenty minutes," Sam said, "not that I'm impatient."

"Just grand," Felicity returned. "I'll be ready in ten."

Sam laughed. "I'm on the way, then. See you soon, Felicity."

"Bye, Sam."

He checked his watch again. Not quite three o'clock. Plenty of time for sightseeing, and Sam knew just where to start. He looked at the tape machine all set up and ready and thought, *It's waited a few days already; it'll keep until later.*

He unthreaded the tape and rewound it back on its spool before locking all the tapes back in the safe. Then he wheeled the machine on its cart back to the Teletype closet and locked it away as well. He retrieved his pistol, put on his safari jacket and hat, and grabbed his cane. Whistling a jaunty tune, Sam headed out for what promised to be an entertaining afternoon.

* * * *

Sam parked his car in the shade of an avocado tree near the ruins of the cathedral bell tower. He got out and went around to the other side to open Felicity's door. She was gracious enough to wait until Sam came around to give her a hand out.

Felicity glanced at Sam, then at the ancient tower, before letting her eyes roam the stone ruins surrounding it that marched silently, almost secretively, away in all directions shrouded beneath massive trees.

While Felicity stared in wonder, a small boy, a street urchin carrying a tin pail of water and sporting a dirty towel on his shoulder, shyly approached the tall gringo and the beautiful rubia.

Sam spoke to him before the boy could make his pitch about guarding and washing Sam's Ford Coupe.

"Cuida mi coche, joven?" Sam proposed.

"Por supuesto, señor!" the boy answered.

"Y lavalo tambien?" Sam asked.

The boy set down his bucket and said enthusiastically, "A lo major, caballero!"

Sam reached into his pocket and handed the kid a half dollar. "Lo diré una otra en mi regreso. Esta bien?"

The boy stared at the silver coin for a second before stuffing it deeply and securely into his pocket. Money now and money later? Such bounty! "Gracias, señor. Mil gracias!"

Sam tousled the boy's hair and gave him a smile. Then he took Felicity gently by the elbow and gestured to the gutted coral block tower as he led her in that direction.

"Handiwork of one of your fellow countrymen," he remarked.

Felicity gave him a quizzical look. With his cane, Sam pointed toward the tower and then to the ruins all around.

"This is the site of the original city—the Old City of Panamá—Panamá Viejo. Founded in 1519 by Pedro Avila De Arias and sacked by the English pirate Captain Henry Morgan in 1671."

They were underneath the tower now and had to crane their heads to look up to the top. Felicity glanced first at Sam and then all about.

"This is utterly incredible," she said in a hushed voice. "Incredible in the truest sense of the word, as in, unbelievable."

Sam gestured across the street to the expanse of overgrown ruins that disappeared into the enfolding forest. "The devastation was so complete that the surviving citizens abandoned the site and moved the city to its current, more defensible, location."

Felicity gazed around in fascination, taking it all in, as Sam led her deeper into the ruined city.

"But they left the city in ruins. Why? Why not reuse the stones for construction at the new site?" she asked. "I know that was done quite often in antiquity."

"I think they left it just the way it was to remind themselves of the perfidy of the English. You see, Spain and England were at peace at the time of the attack. But Morgan burned and sacked the place anyway. And that's in *addition* to all the destruction he wreaked on the Caribbean side of the isthmus where he initially landed."

"Oh my. He was a rogue, wasn't he," Felicity observed.

"That, he certainly was. The Spanish crown screamed to high heavens at the atrocities Morgan and his men committed, but it was all to no avail. Morgan was recalled to England, where the king kept him kicking his heels for a while—at least until the heat died down.

"By then, war with Spain had broken out again, whereupon Morgan was knighted and sent back to Jamaica as lieutenant governor. All to threaten the Spanish in case they took it into their heads to exact retribution."

Felicity looked at Sam. "You admire him, don't you? Morgan, that is. I can hear it in your voice."

Sam gave her a sideways glance. "Oh, I suppose so—in a way. He was a man of bold and audacious action...a man who dared great deeds and operated on a remarkably vast scale. I admire his daring and adventurous spirit."

"Even though he was a pirate?" she asked, a glint of humor in her eye.

"Even though he was a pirate," Sam answered. "Even though he destroyed what was—at that time—one of the greatest, richest cities in all of the Americas."

Sam and Felicity walked awhile in what felt like quiet reverence, treading softly among the silent, brooding ruins and the ancient ghosts that lived among them.

After a while, Felicity broke the silence. "The boy back there, where we parked. What was that all about?"

Sam chuckled before saying, "Lesson number one in Panamá, Felicity. When you park your car, no matter where, there will always be a boy who offers to guard it for you. If he has a bucket, he will also offer to wash it. Always tell him yes. Pay him half the agreed-upon fee up front and make it clear to him that there's more when you return."

"Or?"

"Or you won't like what you find later on," Sam said with a wry grin.

"That sounds to me very much like extortion."

"Oh, I suppose it is, on a miniature scale. But much like all good business transactions, it's worth it for both parties involved."

They walked a bit more before Felicity spoke again. "When you spoke to him, the boy, and with the Panamanians I overheard you with the other night, you sound just like them. Your accent, I mean; your inflection. I speak French fluently, but there's no mistaking I'm English. You must have been here quite some time. You speak the language like a native."

"That's because I am," Sam replied.

Felicity looked puzzled. "But you told me you are a Zonie—an American citizen living in Panama."

"Well, I am that too," he said.

"So you claim to be both at one and the same time. Do you care to explain?"

Sam stopped, turned his head to her, and smiled teasingly. "Full disclosure, Felicity? Is that what you're after? The hidden story of my secret self?"

She tossed her head and laughed, the sound as full-throated as the tenor bells from the old cathedral so many centuries ago. "Only that, Sam. Only that—and your soul!"

Sam laughed and gave her, this time, a quizzical look of his own before taking her arm again and leading her on. Now he spoke seriously.

"My father came here during the canal construction as director of the Smithsonian Institute's newly established tropical research center in Panamá. I was born here. I grew up here; went to school and university here. Other than during the war, Panamá has always been my home."

"I see," Felicity said. "Something like the British in India."

"Maybe. I suspect there are similarities."

"But the Anglo-Indians always thought of themselves as English and of England as their home."

"Most Zonies feel that way about the States too," Sam said.

"But not you?"

He was silent for a bit, thinking. "I'm an American citizen, if that's what you mean."

"But where is your heart? Where is your allegiance? In which country does your soul reside?"

Sam shook his head slightly. "You pose an interesting question. I've never really given it a lot of thought before. Here? The States? Both? Yes, I'd have to say, both."

"You told me of your father. Your mother, was she Panamanian?"

Sam stopped and gave her a hard, sober look. "She was American."

"Was?"

"Yes, my birth mother was. Is. I never knew her. She was a student at Wellesley College. She came to Panamá as a summer intern with the Smithsonian. Met my father, a much older man, and was stricken with what ultimately resulted in me."

"Did she? Is she...?"

"Dead? Oh no, she's very much alive. She stayed here until I was born and then returned to the States, to her home and family in Connecticut."

"Connecticut?" Felicity asked.

"It's one of those northern states, adjacent to New York. She eventually married a banker who is now a U.S. senator. They have three daughters—my half-sisters."

Felicity stopped and faced him. "Do you know her, Sam? Have you met her?"

Sam shook his head. "Just before my father died, he gave me her name and told me the story of my birth. He had kept tabs on her over the years; knew her married name, address, and the names of her other children. He asked that, should I wish to contact her, I wait until he was gone."

"And did you? Contact her?"

"Yes. I wrote her a long letter. I told her of my life and about the years of my father's life since the time she had known him. I told her that I held no animosity for her. I said that if she wanted, I would enjoy correspondence with her, but that I would understand if she preferred not to do so."

Sam looked at Felicity from the tail of his eye. "She responded that her time in Panamá, the affair with my father—and of course me—were things she had worked very hard to forget, and that she would be most pleased if I never made contact with her in any fashion whatsoever again."

Felicity put her hand on his. "Oh Sam. I'm so sorry. I didn't mean to pry."

He squeezed her hand and then took her arm and they walked. "There's no need to be sorry. It's not painful for me. It was all for the best."

"But to lose your mother," she said with sympathy.

"But I *had* a mother," Sam spoke up. "She's the reason I speak with a Panamanian accent. Because of her. My Panamanian mother, Amalia."

"Amalia. What a beautiful name! She was the woman who raised you?"

Sam nodded his head. "My father hired her as my wet nurse. She was a girl from the interior, only seventeen at the time. Abandoned and on her own in the city. She had just lost a child and needed a home. By the time I was a year or so old, she and my father wed. She made a home for all three of us."

"You loved her," Felicity said. A statement, not a question.

"Yes I did, very much. And when she and my father married, under Panamanian law, both he and I became Panamanian citizens."

"Where is she now?" she asked.

"She sleeps beside my father. They're both gone now. She died in '38 and my father joined her in '45."

"So now it's just you," Felicity stated.

"Just me."

"Have you ever married?" she asked casually.

Sam looked over with a small grin. "The answer is, no. And you *do* ask a lot of questions, don't you?"

"When I'm interested," she replied mildly.

Sam made no comment. There was a pause as they continued to walk. After a while, Felicity posed a new question. "Now an easy one, Sam. From whence came the eye patch and the cane? Very stylish, both, I might add!"

"Now that *is* an easy one. They were going-away gifts from a Japanese machine gunner."

"Oh Sam! You say that as lightly as though you were reporting yesterday's weather. Where were you? How did it happen?" she asked excitedly.

"It was in northern Burma, near the Chinese border. I was an advisor with a group of Shan guerillas. We were making an attack on a Japanese outpost. I was hit in the right leg. As I fell, a flying stone chip took out my left eye. That pretty much brought the war to an end for me."

"And when was that?" The excitement was gone, replaced by sadness.

"Early April, '45. Turns out I was quite lucky. The hospital ship they put me on was bound for the East Coast of the States via the canal. When we arrived in Panamá I asked to be debarked here for recovery in the army hospital. Fortunately, my request was granted."

"You say you were lucky. It doesn't sound as if."

"Oh, but I was. I was able to be with my father in his final months. I was here to bury him. Had I not been wounded, I would not have been here for him before the war ended."

Oh, I see. Yes, fortunate in one sense—but still. I'm sorry."

"Nothing of it." Sam waved the thought away. "Now it's your turn, Lady Swathmore. What's your story? What is the fateful route that has graced us with your presence in Panamá?"

She looked down at the ground. "Marriage, I should say."

"If I may be so blunt, yours seems an odd paring. The age difference and all," Sam said.

Felicity's laugh had a sardonic edge to it. "You *do* speak your mind, don't you?

"When I'm interested, I do."

"Ah, touché," she breathed.

"Touché," Sam said with a small smile.

"It's quite simple, actually. An old and honorable British custom. My family desired the Swathmore title and Lord Harrold desired my family's money. You know—impoverished aristocrat marries sole female heiress and all live happily ever after."

"I get it that family money and family titles both desire security and pedigree *for* their offspring, but they also usually want future descendants and offspring—someone to inherit that family money and title. From what little I've seen of this equation, Felicity, that seems a long shot for you—children, I mean."

Felicity gave Sam a startled look, but then her features relaxed. "There does exist that part of the arrangement. I would love to have children, but so far...well...Harrold hasn't...he isn't..." Her voice trailed off.

Sam stopped abruptly and faced her. He took both her arms in his hands. "Don't go on, please, Felicity. That was unfair of me. I had no right to pry into your private life. And I'd rather not hear any details. As a matter of fact, I don't want to know a *damn* thing about your marriage. I only want to know about you."

They looked at each other for what seemed like a long time. Felicity, at last, turned her head away and said, "Sam, I think we should return now."

Sam took her again by the elbow and turned about. "I think you're right. I do have some work on my desk yet."

When they arrived close to the car, Sam looked around for his young guard boy. He was nowhere in sight. *Where's that kid gotten off to? He knew I was coming back with more money,* he wondered. *And it takes a lot to scare a street kid away from money. So where is he? Taking a leak? Maybe he's napping in the shade and he'll come running when he hears the car crank up.*

Sam led Felicity to the passenger side and opened her door. When she was in, he circled the back of the car working his way to the driver's side, hoping to spot the boy somewhere in that direction. As he walked around the rear of the vehicle, Sam froze in his tracks as hard as if he'd run into an invisible wall.

Sitting perfectly centered in the middle of the trunk lid was a dark, round shape. Maybe the size of a bowling ball, but slightly elongated. Darker at the top than at the bottom. Sam took a few steps closer.

Now he was sure what he was looking at: a human head. And unless Sam was seriously mistaken, it was the missing head of Willis Moffitt.

Quickly, smoothly, and hoping Felicity would not turn and see what he was doing, Sam slipped out of his safari jacket. He folded it over and around the grisly head. Holding the damp bundle carefully in one hand, he opened the trunk and placed the jacket and its surprisingly heavy contents into a box storing road flares and emergency equipment. Then he carefully closed the trunk and walked to the driver's door, unconsciously wiping his hands on his trousers.

Sam paused by the door a few seconds, looking around. He hoped to catch sight of the boy. Or perhaps see some sign of whoever had left Willis Moffitt's head perched obscenely on the trunk of his car.

Finally, having spotted nothing, Sam got in, cranked the engine, and pulled rapidly away. The small talk, like the traffic, was sparse as they drove back into town.

* * * *

Sam pulled into the circular drive of the British ambassador's residence, stopped in front of the walkway, and switched off the engine. He got out and opened the car door for Felicity, giving her his hand as he helped her out.

Felicity held Sam's hand lightly, casually, in hers. "Thank you for a lovely outing, Samuel."

"The first of many others, I hope."

She smiled in reply, started to speak, then became serious and said, "A last question, Sam?"

"I have time for just one," Sam grinned.

"In which language do you dream?"

Sam was puzzled. "What?"

"When you dream. What language is it in? Spanish or English?"

He absently touched his eye patch. "Why, English. No—Spanish. Well, actually, I don't know. I've never thought of it before. Both I guess. Why? Does it make a difference?"

"I think it says a lot about who you are," she said levelly.

"And what is that, may I ask?" His eyebrow shot up.

"I think it says you are a man who is caught, who is suspended, between two very different cultures—two very different nations. I think it means you are a man who will be forced, at some point in his life, to declare a clear and single allegiance. And I think when that time comes about, it will be a tortuous decision for you to make."

Sam stared at her and then smiled. He lifted her hand to his lips for a kiss of parting.

"Lady Swathmore, you give a man pause to think. On many different subjects. May I call again?"

"I would like that, Sam. I would like that very much."

"There's racing at the Hippodrome next Friday. Would you care to attend?"

"One of your three passions, isn't it?" she said with a flirtatious smile.

"One of the lesser ones, yes," he replied in kind.

"I'd love to. Goodbye, Sam."

Sam gave her hand a parting squeeze. "Goodbye, Felicity."

Sam watched appreciatively as Felicity continued the flirt with a hip-flung sashay up the walkway to the ambassador's residence. Then he shook off his delight to return to his car and the macabre cargo he carried in the trunk.

He stopped at a pay phone a few blocks away. First he called the office. Cholo told him that Don Julio had reported no strange faces around the neighborhood and no sight of a green Hudson in the area. Sam told him to hang around until he returned.

Next he rang Rivera's headquarters and spoke with the duty officer. He impressed it upon the young lieutenant that it was imperative he find Major Rivera and the gringo officer—find them immediately, wherever they were—and tell them to meet Señor Spears at the Gorgas morgue.

A half-dozen blocks later Sam found himself sitting in his car, stuck in traffic, watching a protest march wend its way slowly down the street. *This is unique,* Sam thought. *This must be what Jorge had hinted at. As a tactic it's positively brilliant! A protest march by an untouchable class of citizens.*

Sam watched admiringly as a large crowd composed entirely of mothers and grandmothers, several hundred at least; all of them dressed in white polleras, the Panamanian national costume. They marched along, loudly beating pots and pans, shouting, "Release my children! What shame! Justice!" and carrying banners that read the same thing:

SUELTAN MIS HIJOS!
QUÉ VERGUENZA!
JUSTICIA!

A Guardia member stood nearby and watched impassively. Sam knew without a doubt that no matter what he was ordered to do, that officer would cut off his own hand before he would wade in with his nightstick to break up that particular group of protesters.

"Well done, ladies," Sam said with admiration. "You've certainly called Arosemena's 'no protest' bluff. And there's not a damn thing he can do about it."

Sam edged his way out of traffic, turned his car around in the middle of the street, and drove off to find a way around. He was in a hurry to get to Gorgas before Rivera and Driscoll arrived.

DOCE

Sam told neither Major Rivera nor Walter Driscoll what he had been doing at Panamá Viejo or with whom. He merely implied he had been there for some kind of a meeting.

The important fact was that he had been followed. By someone with very good tradecraft and by someone connected with Moffitt's death. Sam also felt that the green Hudson, or its driver/occupant, figured into the equation.

"No, Walter, I didn't see anyone other than the boy I told you of," Sam said before he turned and spoke to Rivera. "I think it would be a good idea to send one of your men back out there to see if he can find the kid. I'm hoping whomever it was that left the head on my car just paid the boy to go away instead of strangling him and dumping the body in the river."

"We've no time for that," the major said. "The boy is alive and well, or he is not."

"But he may be able to give us a description of someone," Driscoll mentioned.

"True, Walt. But I've an idea there is more than one person involved," said Sam. "And if that's so, one ran the kid off before the other left his calling card."

"But first, Mr. Driscoll—there is no doubt that this is the body of your man, is that so?" Rivera asked.

All three men looked at the head, sitting upright next to the severed neck of the corpse.

Driscoll shook his head. "There is no doubt. This is Willis Moffitt."

Sam turned to Major Rivera. "Jesús, if there's no objection on your part, I'd like to make arrangements to have the body shipped back to the States."

Rivera shook his head sadly and continued to stare at the corpse, as though there were answers yet to be found there. "I have no objections, Sam. I don't need the body to continue the murder investigation. Send this poor unfortunate one home to his family."

"Thank you, Jesús," Sam said.

"But I think there is more than you are telling me, Sam," said Rivera as he shifted his eyes smoothly from the dead body to Sam's face. "I think this is very much more than a simple murder, spectacular as it may be. Decapitations in Panamá are rare, but not unheard of. In my experience it is a crime of deepest passion. And it is always a message—a message that says, 'This person has violated a sacred trust, and I, the killer, have exacted the appropriate level of vengeance. I have administered justice.'"

"Or a message to others," Driscoll interjected. "An act meant to terrorize—to warn anyone else of the consequences of a certain act."

"There's truth in what you both say," Sam said. "But don't discount the fact that this might have been done by a good old-fashioned madman. Crazy acts are usually performed by crazy people."

"Who knows, Sam? My bet is that Moffitt was a homosexual and was caught up in some sort of homosexual-communist ring. That would explain a lot," Driscoll remarked sourly.

Sam smiled inwardly. He knew FBI types: Hoover clones to a man. Even former ones like Walter Driscoll came away from the Bureau obsessed with the idea of homosexuals and communists as the main sources of all unexplained crimes and conspiracies. It was a notion that in Sam's experience had proven to be an illusion.

"Okay, Walter. You're the ace investigator here, not me," Sam said with a shake of his head. "But we still have the question of: where the hell is Chambers? Anything turn up on that end, Jesús?"

"We ran down the reports of a few pelirojos—redheaded gringos. But in each instance it was someone from the Canal Zone—not your redhead. And we've checked all hospitals, jails, and morgues. He is in none of those."

"I believe when we find Chambers we'll have our answer to this," Sam said, pointing to Moffitt's body.

"He could have left the country," Driscoll added. "Flown, taken a ship, or got on a bus."

"If so, he has not gone through a border control point," said Rivera. "My men are on the lookout; it would have been reported."

Sam tapped his cane on the floor. "Well, gentlemen. It's been a long day and I still have a few things to do. If we have nothing else at the moment, what say we reconvene at a later time?"

"Good idea," said Driscoll.

"Then I bid you both a good evening," Major Rivera said as he turned and departed.

Sam put a restraining hand on Driscoll's arm and waited to speak until Rivera had gone. "Anything at all today, Walt? Anything new turn up that you didn't want to say in front of Rivera?"

Driscoll shook his head. "This case baffles me, Sam. Not a damn thing has turned up. Nothing. And I don't believe Chambers fled. I think he's dead too—rotting in the jungle somewhere, or feeding the crabs out at sea. People don't just disappear like this unless the body has been disposed of or carefully hidden."

"Had the personnel files and photos come in before you left the office?"

Driscoll shook his head again. "No, hopefully we'll have them by tomorrow."

"Perhaps," Sam said. "But no matter what, I want you back on the island tomorrow. I have two new guards laid on, a couple of good men I've known a long time. They'll be going out with you."

"Sounds good, Sam. I don't like this town. And the more I see of it, the less I like it. I'm ready to get back to the island."

“Okay, Walt. Let’s meet at the airfield tomorrow at ten hundred hours.”

“Sure, Sam. Ten it is.”

Sam Spears and Walter Driscoll left the morgue, leaving Willis Moffitt’s mortal remains reunited and homeward bound.

Sam returned to his office and found Cholo still patiently waiting. He asked his friend to round up Turner and Sims in the morning and have them at Albrook Field for a ten o’clock departure to Contadora. Cholo nodded in the affirmative and left.

Sam started to lock up but then had a thought. He went to the Teletype closet to see if any messages had arrived. Sure enough, there were several. He scooped them up and carried them to his desk, where he sat down and leafed through them.

The first two items were the personnel files for Moffitt and Chambers—mostly dry data, nothing really helpful other than photos of the men. But the pictures, he knew, would aid in the search for Chambers and the quest for Moffitt’s movements before his murder.

The last message, however, gave Sam a surprise. It didn’t take long to decode, as it was quite succinct and to the point. It read:

> GOTTLIEB INTERROGATIONS TO RECOMMENCE. SPEARS RELIEVED OF ALL OVERSIGHT AND MANAGEMENT RESPONSIBILITY. DRISCOLL ASSUMES LOCAL COMMAND OF PROJECT ARTICHOKE.
> ...CARLETON BROADSTREET

Sam leaned back in his chair. “Jesus Hotel Christ,” he said. He poured himself a shot of bourbon, propped his aching leg on the desk, and lit a cigar. Thinking. Carleton Broadstreet wasn't the one who had made the decision to restart the chemical interrogations. He didn't have the authority. Only the committee overseeing Project Artichoke, as it was called, could do that. But Carleton had made sure the order went out under his name. That, in itself, was a message Sam should be alert for trouble and proceed as he saw fit.

But what was fit? That was the salient question. The easiest course of action would be to simply obey orders, wash his hands of Contadora, and forget it. It wasn't as if he didn't have other responsibilities. Hell, the Russians were circling the isthmus like vultures over a dead carcass. And Villanueva's story about the upcoming Panamanian presidential election was sure to be no more than an elaborate fiction.

Sam gathered the papers in a manila folder and locked them away in the safe. He went to the sideboard in his office and took out a five-cigar tin of Macanudos. He opened the can and selected a cigar. Working very carefully, he slid off the band and placed it on the surface of his desk. With the thin blade of his Case pocket-knife, he worked the seam of the band until it opened and spread flat. On the inside of the band Sam wrote in very small letters the word "Bohica." Then he moistened the band with the tip of his tongue, placed it back around the cigar, and put the cigar back in the tin. He thumbed through his office closet for a new jacket to take the place of his safari jacket befouled by Willis Moffitt's head. It would be a long time before that memory would leave him. He downed the last of the bourbon, put the tin in his jacket pocket, grabbed his hat and cane, and locked up for the night.

* * * *

It was just after midnight when Sam pulled into his drive and turned off the engine. As he stepped onto the walkway leading across the lawn to his house, he noticed that the nightlights over his front porch as well as those along the front walkway were out.

At least it's nearly a full moon tonight, he thought as he fished his house keys from his pocket. *Must have been a power surge again. I'll get Cholo to send his brother-in-law over tomorrow to replace the bulbs and check the circuit.*

Sam was feeling for the right key to the front door when he fumbled and dropped the whole key ring to the ground.

"Dammit," he swore, bending to retrieve them. But as his fingers touched the keys lying on the walkway, he saw something odd: two thin, dark lines running from side to side across the flagstones. Sam froze. He'd seen this same kind of thing before, in another time and another place. It was not good, and it focused Sam's attention like a microscope.

Sam left the keys where they lay and placed his cane across the walkway to serve as a limit marker. Then he stood, calmly drew his pistol, and looked carefully all around. Turning slowly and moving quietly, he went back to his car and got a flashlight from the glove box. Then he returned, and one full pace short of where he had placed his walking stick, he knelt, flicked on the light, and played the beam across the walkway.

Seen from this angle, there was just one line across the walk. In the light of the moon, Sam had also seen the shadow of the thin copper wire that spanned the walkway at ankle height and disappeared into the bushes on either side.

Sam kept his flashlight on the wire and tracked it toward the left side of the walk first. Carefully and gently, using the utmost caution, he pushed aside the leaves of an oleander bush and saw that the wire itself was secured to the main stem of the shrub. He didn't touch the wire but tracked it now toward the right side of the walkway. He put his face down so his eye was level with the pavement and shined his flashlight into the bushes.

When he saw the grenade, Sam was impressed. "My, my! This is a nasty one," he said to himself. "Whoever did this knew exactly what he was doing." Usually with this sort of booby trap—a trip-wired grenade—the grenade was slid down into a tin can and the pin was pulled, with the spoon being held in place by the can itself. The trip wire was attached to the head of the grenade and stretched across the path where someone was likely to walk. When the victim hit the wire, the grenade would be yanked from the can, the spoon would go flying, and the grenade would detonate.

That all went well if you were ambushing a squad of soldiers, because a hand grenade has a five-second fuse. So no matter what, the grenade was sure to get someone. But this particular trip-wire trap was diabolical in the extreme.

This grenade wasn't in a can. It was wedged into a fork of bush and taped into place. The trip wire was inserted through the fuse head where the pin had once been and the wire had been kinked slightly—to give it just enough resistance so that a falling leaf or small twig would not set it off. What made the device so exceedingly dangerous was that the standard hand grenade five-second fuse had been replaced with the quarter-second fuse of a smoke grenade. Had Sam hit the wire, he would have had time for only half a stride, his foot still in the air, before the grenade detonated. It would have blown off his legs and splattered the rest of him across the yard in ugly red pieces.

Sam placed the flashlight on the ground so that its ray shined fully on the grenade. He then pulled the kinked end of the wire as far as he could and wrapped it around the fuse head. Next, he went to the other side of the walk, where he carefully detached that end of the wire from the stem of the oleander shrub.

When he returned to the grenade, he took the loose wire and wrapped it, turn after turn, tightly around the body of the grenade and the spoon, binding them securely together and rendering the device safe. At last he took out his pocketknife and cut the grenade free from its nest.

Putting the grenade in his jacket pocket, he took his flashlight and carefully searched the walkway up to the house and across the porch to the door. Satisfied all was clear, he went inside and made his way straight to the servant's quarters to awaken Gloria. She was a little deaf these days. She also liked to have a shot or two of rum before going to bed, so it took a while for her to respond to Sam's insistent knocking.

The elderly housekeeper was none too happy about being gotten up in the middle of the night and she let Sam know it. She grumbled and complained bitterly, but finally did as Sam asked and packed a small bag. He drove her across town to the colonia of San Miguelito to stay with one of her granddaughters for a few days. That good lady and her family were also confused as to why Sam was dropping their abuela off at such an ungodly hour. But as everyone in Panamá knew from long experience—gringos were strange people. Even those who, like Sam, spoke Spanish and had lived there their entire lives.

On his return from San Miguelito, Sam stopped on the waterfront of Avenida Balboa. He parked, then walked across the avenue and stepped to the railing at the water's edge. He looked up and down the roadway and waited for a lone taxi to pass by.

When the taxi's taillights had diminished to small red dots, Sam reached in his jacket pocket for the grenade. He reared back, took a step forward, and with his best fastball delivery hurled the deadly steel lump a good fifty yards out to sea. It hit the water with a muted splash and plummeted to the muddy bottom. Sam knew the twice daily tide, which ran as much as fifteen feet, would soon work the nasty little bugger down into the sand and silt of the bay floor. The salt water would eat the fuse head away and that would be the end of it. The grenade would rest in safety.

Even if it were to go off, it would only kill a few fish—and some lucky boy would scoop them up to carry home for supper, Sam thought as he crossed the empty street. *But no matter what, I'm going to find the bastard who left that little welcome home present. And when I do...*

Sam got back into his car and pulled away. He drove the few blocks to the Hotel Centro Americana, where he checked in for the night. Fortunately, they knew him there. Even without baggage.

* * * *

Sam was at his office early the next morning. He filled the coffeepot with makings and while it perked he got a brief message off to Carleton Broadstreet confirming receipt of the previous day's orders. He also sent a second, separate message announcing the positive identification of Willis Moffitt's body and the arrangements made for shipping the remains back to the States. He let Broadstreet know that Chambers was still missing but that the hunt for his whereabouts continued. Then he turned off the telex machine and locked the door to its closet.

He checked his watch and realized it was still too early to head over to Albrook, so he poured himself a coffee and took it to his desk. From the corner he wheeled the tape machine close to his desk, retrieved the bag of tapes from his safe, and threaded the first reel into the device. He turned the switch to activate the device, picked up his cup of coffee, and leaned back in his chair to listen.

The machine hummed for a few seconds and then began to emit a loud series of hisses, squeals, and crackling static. Sam quickly reached over and turned it off. He checked to make sure he had set everything up correctly and turned the machine on again.

Same result: hiss, crackle, pop. Nothing. Sam stopped the tape and ran it forward; stopped and listened again. Same thing. He ran all the way through the tape, stopping and listening, before rewinding and listening again. There was nothing there. The interrogation tape contained nothing but electronic racket. He went through all the other tapes with no better luck.

Sam looked coldly at the reels of tape scattered across the top of his desk. *Garbage. Nothing here but garbage. But who had done it? Who had erased these tapes and why? Was it Driscoll?* Sam wondered.

He knew Driscoll hadn't been too happy about handing the tapes over to begin with, but he didn't think Driscoll would have done this.

If Walter had a real objection to turning over the tapes, he would have refused to do it and messaged for instructions from headquarters. No, whoever did this did it without Driscoll's knowledge. Besides—they were making a point. They wanted me to know the erasure was no accident.

Sam wheeled the tape machine back to its corner and poured more coffee. For good measure, he dosed it with bourbon. Then he sat down and made a mental review of everything that had taken place on the island from the beginning of the project until this very moment. When he finished his musings, Sam knew that he had just hit a trip wire of his own.

He unlocked his personal safe and took out several boxes. From one of these he pulled out an old, very worn leather wallet and put it on his desk. From the other boxes he chose a number of items, which he also laid out on the desk.

He opened the wallet and tucked inside it things he was still sorting out from among the items he had laid out on the desk. Five hundred dollars in old bills went into the cash slip. A faded nine of clubs playing card, torn in half, was stored in a slip for a photograph. A sheaf of four rare stamps he had picked up with a pair of tweezers and inserted in a glassine envelope was put into a pocket of the wallet.

He shuffled through several blank identity cards before selecting two of them. He took these into Marta's office and inserted the first one into the typewriter and typed steadily, filling in the empty spaces. He did the same with the other card.

Sam returned to his desk and to each of the cards he glued an identical photo chosen from a small stack of photographs stored in one of the boxes. When the glue had set, he picked out an embossing stamp and made a seal across the photo on each card. Then he signed a signature beneath each photograph and inspected his work with a magnifying glass. Satisfied with his forgery, he put the new identity cards in the wallet and tucked the wallet itself into the breast pocket of his new jacket.

Finally, he gathered together all the items spread across the desk and returned them to their respective boxes. The boxes, along with the erased tapes, he returned to the safe.

Sam stood and looked around the room as though taking it in for one last time. He took his hat and cane and headed for the door, missing his much-loved old safari jacket. He had the doorknob in hand when he had another thought and turned back into the room. He went back to the sideboard and pulled the plug on the coffeepot. One last look and Sam left the office for Albrook Airfield.

Outside, as he unlocked his car, he noticed a slip of paper tucked beneath the driver's side wiper blade. Sam looked carefully around the area before plucking the doubled-over slip and opening it. He scanned the note and chuckled to himself as he refolded and pocketed it.

"So, matters progress," he said, relocking the Coupe. He touched his head in exasperation as if he'd forgotten something and headed back inside the office.

Sam hurriedly opened his safe and took out a large manila folder. He thumbed through the contents of the folder until he found a clipped sheaf of papers. Satisfied he had the material he needed, he locked the safe, sealed the sheaf of papers in a large envelope from Marta's office, and went out again to meet the day.

Since he still had some time, he stopped on the way at a small café on the waterfront. A place owned by the Greek Marakopoulos family, friends he had helped come to Panamá as refugees after the war. There Sam had a quiet and leisurely American-style breakfast while he considered events, and his next moves, with a sense of calm optimism.

TRECE

Sam took the tin of Macanudos from his jacket and handed them to Walter Driscoll. "I promised Demitrova I would send him some of these when I got the chance. Would you make sure he gets them?"

Driscoll took the flat tin of luxury cigars and looked at them with surprise. "Sam, we have tobacco on the island. You know the inmates aren't allowed this sort of thing—it's contraband. It's against regulations."

"Hell, Walt," Sam said with a conspiratorial grin. "He asked me to smuggle him a bottle of whiskey and a woman! You know I was never one to bend the rules too much. And maybe, in a small way, it will help to smooth Demitrova's ruffled feathers. I think this is the very least I can do."

Driscoll laughed. "Sam, you never saw a symbol of authority that you didn't feel compelled to challenge. But yes, I'll see that he gets them," he said as he placed the cigars in his pocket.

Sam glanced over his shoulder. The plane was idling on the apron, Turner and Sims already aboard. "Well, you better get on with it. Now that you're in charge, you'll want to get back and take things in hand. You have any questions or need anything from me, you know where I am."

Driscoll picked up the briefcase sitting at his feet and then extended his hand. "Thanks, Sam. I'm glad you're not taking this hard. It'll make things go a lot easier this way."

Sam returned the shake. "To tell the truth, it's a relief to me, Walt. I've got other fish to fry. Now, go on, before Gaddis leaves without you."

Driscoll looked at Sam with a combination of respect and relief, then ducked his head and trotted to the waiting plane. As soon as the door was closed, Gaddis had them heading down the runway. Within two minutes the plane was gaining altitude and turning south out over the mouth of the canal.

Sam waited until the plane was out of sight and then joined Cholo Martinez, who had stood by, waiting quietly. He told him what had happened the night before at his home. "Don't go near there. I've taken Gloria to her daughter's, and I'll make arrangements to have the place watched."

Cholo nodded in understanding. "What you want me to do?" he asked.

"First thing," Sam said, handing over a set of keys, "make sure the boat has full tanks and then move her to the landing at Diablo. In my boat shed there, you'll find that old footlocker that we set up when we made the trip to Colombia last year. Check to make sure everything is in it that's supposed to be and then put it in the cabin."

Cholo pocketed the keys. "I will make sure everything works and put new cartuchos in footlocker—old ones been there too long, I think."

"Good idea. Once that's done, I'd like you to go to the office and stay there. There's a cot in my office closet. Get some food and drink and set yourself up for a few days."

"I stay 'til you tell me go," Cholo replied.

"I don't think it will be for very long. I'll contact you when I can," Sam said.

"Okay, Sam."

"And one other thing. Remind Don Julio to keep an eye out for that Hudson. Tell him if it's spotted to have it followed. But above all, get me a description of the driver."

Cholo nodded again and replied, "Entiendo."

Cholo climbed into the Willys and pulled away. Sam followed in his Ford. At the Albrook gate, they turned in different directions.

* * * *

The corporal announced, "You have a visitor, sir."

Captain Stephen J. Harris, company commander of the Fort Clayton Military Police, looked up from his desk. When he saw Sam, he got hurriedly to his feet.

Sam waved him back to his chair. "No, please, Captain. I'm the intruder here. Forgive me for barging in unannounced, but I have a problem that I hope you can help me with."

Captain Harris indicated a chair and waited until Sam was seated before he settled again behind his desk. "Major, if it's at all within my power to assist you, please be assured that I will."

Sam gave the MP captain a carefully edited version of the incident at his house the previous evening and asked if he could post an MP jeep and a couple of men in his drive for the next few days.

"I don't think it will be for very long, Captain. And the men don't need to patrol or anything; their presence will be sufficient. I would normally use Canal Zone Police for this, but I think just the sight of army MPs makes for a much better deterrent."

It was an easy decision for Captain Harris. A chance to do something—anything—for the legendary Major Spears was an honor.

"I'll have a team posted by sixteen hundred hours, if that's all right with you, sir. And we'll maintain the post until you say otherwise," said Captain Harris, with a swell of pride at being called to action.

Sam rose and gave Harris his hand. "Thank you, Captain. You don't know how much I appreciate this. And I promise to tell you more about it all when matters have concluded."

Harris returned the handshake. "Just glad to help, sir."

Sam touched a forefinger to his brow in salute and departed. Captain Harris sat back at his desk, feeling important and needed. For a change.

* * * *

The Guardia lieutenant escorted Sam across the dining room to a table with a lone occupant. The lieutenant came to attention and spoke to the imposing man at the table.

"Señor Spears, mi comandante."

Colonel José Antonio Remón Cantera, commander of La Guardia Nacional de La Republica de Panamá, studied Sam from beneath lowered brows. Cantera was a heavily built man in his early forties, with very fair skin, a round face, and piercing intelligent eyes. His manner was mild, even benign, but Sam knew that his looks deceived.

The Guardia commander was an iron fist in a velvet glove; you crossed this man at your peril. He had led at least one coup d'état already and had ousted two additional presidents by other means. If there were a Big Chief on the isthmus, it was Colonel Remón. And today, he and Sam were going to make medicine.

Colonel Remón gestured to the only other chair at the table and said in a surprisingly high-pitched voice, "Join me, sir."

As Sam sat, waiters rushed up and served the table.

"I took the liberty of ordering for us," remarked Remón. "I know your time is precious, and I wanted to squander little of it."

"I thank you for the invitation, Colonel. I did not expect such a prompt response to my request."

A waiter placed a drink on the table for Sam. Remón lifted his own glass. "Salvador Libre, that is your drink, is it not, Mr. Spears?"

Sam picked up the glass and took a sip. He nodded his appreciation. "Sabrosisimo! Colonel, you are the perfect host."

"Your favorite drink...." Remón then indicated the plates. "Your favorite meal. Where you live. What you do. Where you go, your family history, even your war record. There's little I don't know about you, Señor Spears."

Sam put his glass back on the table and looked at the commander. "My life is an open book, Colonel. I live in a glass house."

"In which case, one should avoid throwing stones."

"Stones, sir?" Sam inquired.

"Stones. Loose talk. A prudent man, a careful man, avoids both," Remón said evenly.

"I couldn't agree more, sir. Intentional or not, they can cause great harm," said Sam with a tight smile.

Remón looked from the settings on the table to Sam. "Buen provecho, Señor Spears." Remón picked up a fork and gave his attention to the meal. Sam followed suit.

* * * *

Two busboys cleared the table as a waiter poured coffee. Sam offered his host a cigar. Remón nodded his thanks as he accepted. Sam extended his Ronson and gave the colonel a light before lighting his own. The men took a few appreciative puffs, smoking, thinking, and eyeing one another. Two jaguars sizing potential prey.

"Cards on the table, señor?" Remón asked.

Sam waved a hand—*yes*.

"Arosemena thinks I plot against his government."

"Does he now? Wherever would he get such an idea?" Sam asked, reaching up to adjust the edge of his eye patch.

"Quite possibly from you, I suspect," said Remón with a dash of humor in his voice.

"Well," Sam replied slowly. "A bit of tension in politics is never entirely amiss. But let me pass on the feelings of my people, sir. Your candidacy for president, should that come about, would be looked upon with great favor in Washington."

Remón studied his cigar before replying, "I am gladdened to hear that."

"However, there is one fly in the ointment," Sam added.

Remón asked casually, "And what might that be?"

"Villanueva, as your running mate, as candidate for vice president. That is something that would create all manner of problems."

"What sort of problems would those be?" Remón asked mildly.

Sam took the envelope of papers from beneath his jacket and slid them across the table. "These sorts of problems, mi Colonel. The ones you'll find in these documents. Dealings with the Russians—dealings, I'm sure, that neither you nor your own intelligence service are aware of."

Remón glanced disdainfully at the envelope and made no move to pick it up or even touch it. "Documents can be forged. Written material is not proof of anything, Señor Spears."

"Very true," Sam replied. "These are merely the transcripts of taped recordings between Foreign Minister Villanueva and his secret contact at the Soviet embassy in Mexico City. A man named Anatoly Lavrov."

Sam nudged the envelope closer to Colonel Remón's hand. "After reading these, should you have more questions, I will be happy to supply the original, unedited tapes. And after you've made certain that the information contained here is indeed true, there's one other thing I think both sides would like to see happen."

"And that is?" Remón asked.

"That Villanueva be charged with treason."

Remón looked from Sam to the papers and back to Sam. "Treason. That is such an...ugly word."

"Colonel, you'll notice I did not say 'indicted' or 'tried' but rather 'charged.'" He leaned forward. "Let the press and public opinion do its work. Villanueva is too much of a power to have in the Remón administration. You'll need at least a year, maybe two, to consolidate your political position. You'll want your own people, men loyal to you and you alone, in the places of leverage.

"Jorge Villanueva, as vice president, would spend his time plotting to supplant you. It's a matter of class and family, mi Colonel. Villanueva is a member of the haves. That handful of families who have always run things. While you, sir, are of the have-nots. And please don't think they will ever forget that fact—not for a second. In fact, it will goad them into opposing you at every turn. But a politically castrated Villanueva is in both our best interests. A charge of treason would discredit not only him but also his entire family and his supporters. Villanueva would be completely neutralized as an opponent."

Colonel Remón stared off into the distance as he mouthed the cigar smoke and blew contemplative rings into the air. At last, he looked at Sam, jaguar to jaguar, and said, "I have greatly enjoyed this opportunity to break bread together and share a few thoughts, Señor Spears. I would hope, in the future, we are able to do so on a more regular basis."

Sam smiled. "As would I, mi Colonel. As would I."

CATORCE

Sam cruised his boat into the harbor at Taboga Island. He slowly circled the mooring area, checking the flow of the tide and the distance between the other boats. On the outer side of the harbor he admired a beautiful forty-foot ketch, *La Pasa Tiempo,* which looked capable of crossing oceans.

He swung to the inner side of the moorage and dropped anchor near the abandoned nineteenth-century stone wharf of the old Pacific American Steamship Line. Once he was sure his anchor was securely buried in the sandy bottom, he locked the cabin and slid the dinghy over the transom.

The incoming tide gave him a push as he rowed the short distance to shore. Sam pulled the dinghy up above the high-tide mark and stowed the oars away beneath the seat. Taboga was the one place in Panamá you didn't need to post a guard. The island was too small for petty criminals. There was nowhere for a thief to hide. And the ferry to the mainland only ran twice a day so there was no place to go either. Sam slung an old haversack over his shoulder and used his cane to climb the narrow cobblestone footpath that led up from the beach, up through town, and to the old hotel perched high above.

Sam took a room on the lee side of the building; one out of the wind that had a view out over the open Pacific. He gave the bellboy some money and sent him out for ice and drinks. When the boy returned, he gave him a nice tip and asked that he be called when the final ferry of the day arrived in the harbor. Then he made himself a tall, cold drink and took it out to the balcony to lounge in the oversized striped cotton hammock that swung in the shade.

Settled comfortably in the hammock, a pillow doubled up behind his head, he began the book he had brought along: Eric Ambler's novel, *A Coffin for Dimitrios*. Sam didn't usually read noir—he preferred histories—but for some reason or other, this title had caught his eye at the bookstore.

The sun was hot. He felt the sea in the sway of the hammock. He slept without dreams.

Sam woke just as the sun was sliding below the horizon. The bellboy seemed a little surprised and not too happy when Sam opened the door at the first knock. He was worried that since Sam was already awake from his siesta, he'd receive no tip. He'd taken Sam to be a native, and as the boy knew quite well, Panamanians were notoriously tacaño: stingy. But the boy changed his attitude when Sam gave him a silver dollar and a pat on the shoulder for his diligence and sent him happily on his way.

When Sam stepped out of the hotel, he looked down over the town to the harbor and saw the ferry just easing into the dock. He was glad of the aid of his walking stick as he made his descent. His wounded leg usually gave him only a little trouble, but it always made itself known in protest whenever he descended a steep incline or a long flight of stairs, and here he was faced with both.

At last, Sam stood on the walkway just above the landing where he could see over the heads of the crowd and watch as the ferry disgorged a small throng of humanity onto the island. On the late-evening run, most of the disembarking passengers were either those who worked at jobs in the city or had spent the day ashore, visiting or shopping.

Sam scanned the crowd as it dispersed, studying faces and body types. He had taken a position to the side of the walkway so that each passenger had to walk past him on their way up from the public landing. Sam stayed in place until everyone had departed and the ferry was shut down and tied up for the night.

When the crew had also come ashore, Sam ambled down to the dock and took a seat on a bench that looked out over the beach and the harbor beyond. He cupped his hand around the Ronson to protect the flame from the wind and carefully lit a cigar. Sam crossed his legs, laid the end of his walking stick casually over the instep of his foot, and counted the boats moored in the harbor. The number of vessels was the same as when he had dropped anchor that afternoon.

The sky darkened rapidly as Sam sat and smoked. The lights in the city across the bay began to sparkle, and the stars shined brightly in the inky black of the tropical sky. Sam stubbed out his cigar. He rose and ambled back to the other side of town, his stick tapping the paving stones with every other step. With darkness and the cool of the evening, the tiny town of Taboga was just coming alive.

Sam made his way through the narrow street now thronged with families, chatting neighbors, playing children, and strolling lovers. At the end of the beach was a waterside restaurant with tables set in the sand beneath a palm-thatched bohio. When the smiling young waitress arrived, Sam ordered a large ceviche de corvina, fried yuca and patacones, and a Salvador Libre. When she came back with Sam's drink, he found out her name was Marisol. By the time Sam had finished his meal and had a second drink, Marisol happily accepted his gallant offer to walk her home when the restaurant closed and her duties were finished for the evening.

The next morning, he slept late and enjoyed a leisurely breakfast at the hotel. He then walked down to the dock to meet the ferry as it made its return trip from the city. Once again he studied the passengers who came ashore, and just as carefully, he scanned the faces of those who boarded for the trip back to the mainland. Afterward, Sam changed into swim trunks and lazed on the beach, reading his novel and keeping an eye on the harbor for arriving private boats.

He thought about how good the heat of the sun felt; especially so on his wounded leg. Later, when he felt he had absorbed enough rays, he went for a swim. That, too, felt especially good, and he made a promise to himself to take Blanquita for a beach getaway one weekend soon. Maybe up the coast to San Carlos.

When the sun was directly overhead, Sam returned to his hotel for a shower and a light lunch. He then stretched out in the hammock with his book opened over his face and took a long, much-welcomed siesta. He awoke just as the sun touched the horizon.

Sam slung the haversack over his shoulder and, stick in hand, made his way again to the dock, where first he counted the boats in the harbor and then watched the disembarking passengers of the day's last ferry run.

From a vendor on the dock, Sam bought a beer and a dozen empanadas. He ate two of the delicious meat-filled pastries for his evening meal, and the remainder he stowed away in the haversack. He took a seat on the dock bench where he had watched the passengers descend the previous evening. He lit a cigar and sat and smoked until it was fully dark and no one was left on the beach. Then he went down, shoved his dinghy into the water, and rowed out to his boat.

Sam dragged the dinghy up onto the transom and made it snug. He unlocked the cabin and brought out a wooden deck chair that he unfolded and placed near the helm, where he was out of the wind and could prop his feet up on the starboard gunnel. Sam sat quietly, his mind at rest, lulled by the rocking of the boat and the sound of the water gurgling along the hull as the movement of the tide picked up speed.

The sounds of the town had begun to subside. Sam checked his watch and saw that moonrise would be in twenty minutes. He folded the deck chair and stowed it away in the forward cabin. He dragged the footlocker from inside and tucked it away on the port side of the cockpit, where he made it fast with a turn of line. Then he cranked the engine. He watched the panel instruments until the pressures and temperatures were correct before he put the transmission lever in the forward position and gave the accelerator a slight nudge.

As the bow of the boat moved into the wind and tide at idle speed, Sam flipped the toggle switch that controlled the electric anchor winch. The boat moved slowly forward to meet the rising anchor as the winch took in chain and dropped it into the locker below the bow deck. Sam heard the anchor clatter as it rolled up into its cradle and felt the winch groan as it came to a stop.

He flipped off the winch and let the boat continue across the harbor at dead slow. He eased in behind the row of boats nearest the shore and made his way stealthily to the other side of the anchorage. When he came alongside *La Pasa Tiempo,* he shifted into reverse for a second and smoothly brought his boat to a near halt. He snatched a boat hook from beneath a gunnel and, as he drifted past the bow of the pretty sailboat, used the boat hook to snag its mooring line. Then he cut the mooring line and walked it back to his stern, where he deftly tied it to a longer length of rope already coiled and attached to a cleat on the transom.

He let the forward momentum of his boat pay out the line. When it was tight, he went back to the helm, put his boat in gear, and with *La Pasa Tiempo* securely in tow, he eased silently out of the darkened harbor and into the narrow and seldom-used channel between Taboga and its smaller sister island, Taboguilla.

On this side of the island there were no buildings, no lights, and no prying eyes. Once through the channel and in open water, Sam throttled up and set a course of one hundred twenty degrees. He glanced back over his shoulder and saw the moon just beginning to lift its head above the dark mountains of the Continental Divide.

* * * *

Dimitri Demitrova looked again at the playing card that lay on his nightstand. The knave of diamonds. The jack, as the Americans called it. Dimitri wondered why the Americans had so many strange words in their version of English. It was true what Churchill had said about England and America: two peoples separated by a common language.

It was this separation of language that was giving Dimitri difficulty now as he labored to compose his suicide letter. A man's last words should be clear and meaningful, with no ambiguities of misconstruction and no room for misunderstanding.

Dimitri wanted to make perfectly clear the reasons for his action and the man he held directly responsible for what he now did. He had risked everything in coming over to the Americans. And he had been deceived. He had been lied to. He had been played falsely. He had been abused. And all of this he now laid at the feet of the man who had induced him to defect: none other than his erstwhile friend, supposed benefactor, and personal betrayer, Samuel Ransom Spears.

There were two cigars left in the tin on the nightstand. Dimitri lit one and went to stand and smoke at the open door to his room, where he leaned against the doorframe and watched the moon as it began to rise over the mainland.

Two new guards walked across the lawn in front of Dimitri's building. One glanced over in his direction but Dimitri ignored them both. He was no longer concerned with guards. Or camp routine. Or anything else having to do with life on Contadora. Dimitri's mind was made up. And when Dimitri Demitrova reached a decision and settled on a course of action, he could not be deterred.

His cigar now reduced to a stub, he dropped it to the walkway in front of his door and ground it out with the heel of his shoe. He turned back into his room, took up his pen, and began to write.

* * * *

The boat rose and fell, riding the wind-driven waves as it made its way steadily downwind. Sam didn't need to look behind him to know that the moon was now fully risen. He could see its reflection bobbing and dancing brightly on the water ahead.

He scanned his instruments and checked the heading on the compass. The card glowed dimly under the binnacle's red light, and the lubber line showed that he was on course. At a speed of eight knots, and with the aid of a following sea, Sam calculated he would be at his destination in three hours.

He locked the wheel in place with two looped lines, each one on a spoke at opposite sides of the wheel, leaned back in the captain's chair, and scanned the horizon in all directions. Seeing no sign of any other vessel, he flipped a switch on the instrument panel and turned off his boat's navigation lights. He knew very well that a white boat—two white boats, one closely behind the other—cruising smoothly over white-capped waves on a moonlit silver sea would be almost impossible to spot from any distance at all.

* * * *

Dimitri Demitrova walked to his door and checked the position of the moon. It was now almost directly overhead. He went back in.

From the nightstand he picked up the letter he had written, folded it neatly, and tucked it into his shirt pocket. He then smoothed the blanket on his bed and plumped the pillow. Dimitri was a neat man; he didn't want to be remembered as keeping a slovenly room. He took the last cigar from the tin, lit it, and huffed on it to make sure it was going well.

Dimitri had hoarded the vodka that Sam had given him. He picked up the bottle and saw that there was about a centimeter left. He tucked the bottle under his arm, turned out the lights, and left the room, closing the door carefully behind him.

* * * *

In the distance, Sam could just make out the dark line of the island ahead. He took up his binoculars and put an eyepiece to his right eye. He scanned slowly left and right, in an arc of about fifteen degrees, and then he saw it just above the surface of the water: a faint red pinpoint of light, appearing and disappearing erratically in the distance. He put down the binoculars and looked up overhead. A small bite had been taken from the eastern side of the moon. As he watched, that bite grew inexorably larger as the face of the moon was steadily consumed. By a jaguar, if the old legends were true. Sam liked to think that was so.

* * * *

Dimitri Demitrova stood on the end of the dock and faced out to sea. He looked up at the moon. It was now almost totally dark. Sam had deceived him in many things, but he had been right about the eclipse. It was a once in a lifetime event. A sight he would not have wanted to miss. But now it was almost over. Dimitri took a last few puffs from his cigar and then casually flipped the butt to the water. It flew in a vivid red arc, like a miniature meteorite, before splashing to its death with a muted hiss.

He uncapped the vodka bottle and finished it off with one swallow. He put the cap back on the bottle and sat it carefully down on the wooden dock. Then he began to undress. He slipped out of his shoes and set them to one side. He took off his socks, rolled each one neatly, and placed each in its respective shoe. He unbuttoned the fly of his trousers and stepped out of them. These he also folded carefully and placed on the dock. He removed his undershorts and put them atop the trousers. He took off his shirt, folded neatly with breast pocket facing the stars, and placed it uppermost on the stack of clothing. He then sat the empty bottle, as an anchor, on top of the stack, directly over the pocket that held his suicide letter.

Dimitri Demitrova was not a man given to theatrics. When he did something, no matter how momentous, he did it in an offhand manner that acknowledged his truth: *I have committed other deeds in my life, deeds much more difficult than this one.*

Dimitri looked to the sky and watched as the last bit of light was extinguished from the face of the moon. Then he stepped smoothly to the end of the dock, bent forward at the waist, and—extending his arms—dove as far out into the sea as he possibly could.

Dimitri's naked body sliced into the water like the blade of a keen knife. He allowed his momentum to carry him forward in a long underwater glide. And when he finally emerged and broke the surface of the water, he began to swim.

* * * *

Sam brought the boat to idle a hundred yards outside the reef. At that exact moment, the moon went completely black. In the distance he could barely make out the light at the end of the dock, but he could hear the faint sounds of the palms on the shoreline. Fronds flapping and rattling in the wind.

He strained his eye to its utmost as he scanned the water between his boat and the light on the dock. He picked up his GI flashlight with its red filter over the lens and began to blink it in a series of three flashes, a pause, and then three flashes again.

With no headway on, both the boats had turned beam-on into the wind and began to rock with a violent snapping motion. Sam braced his injured leg against the gunnel of the boat. He steadied himself with a hand on the rail, and holding the flashlight high overhead, he blinked the signal over and over again.

Try as he might, Sam was unable to make out anything in the darkness. He lifted a boson's whistle hanging from a chain around his neck and blew three short, shrill blasts—each blast in cadence with the pulses of the flashlight. Then he alternated: three blasts of the whistle followed by three blinks of the light.

* * * *

Demitrova swam steadily on; on and on it seemed, toward the open ocean. He knew he was now outside the cleft in the reef because he felt himself pounded by the full force of the waves. The seas were short, fierce, choppy, and totally without rhythm. Continually, he was driven under, only to surface spitting mouthfuls of water and gasping for air. He sputtered and choked every time his head cleared water. He was beginning to tire.

As his strength waned, Dimitri realized what poor physical condition he was in. But it was a concern that would matter just a bit longer; he needed only to get out to open water. And then, as he lifted his head above the water for a look around, a tall, dark fin sliced the surface only a few feet in front of his face.

"Oh God! Oh God! Oh God!" Dimitri screamed aloud as he kicked leaden legs harder and dug through rock waves with tiring arms. "Please God, please. Not that!" he begged. Dimitri

Demitrova found new energy in his fear, and he swam with every ounce of strength left in his body.

* * * *

Sam heard a noise, perhaps a voice, and then saw a splash. *Yes! There!*

He leapt to the top of the gunnel and held on to the edge of the cabin roof with one hand. He blew his whistle with long, insistent blasts. He flashed his light, over and over again, and yelled above the waves, "Here! Out here! Dead ahead, Dimitri! Come this way! I'm here!"

* * * *

Dimitri heard the whistle first. And then—heaven—Sam's voice.

He looked up. Dancing above the waves he saw the red light blinking straight ahead. Then he made out the shape of the boat.

"Here! Over here! Help me! Here!" Dimitri screamed "God!" as a large black shape raked into him, shearing his flank with the rough skin of its large, high tail.

At last Sam caught sight of him in the water. And as the moon began to emerge again, he also saw the shadow of the shark as it turned and made a tight circle close behind the struggling man.

Sam blew his whistle unceasingly. He leapt from gunnel to the helm and slammed the boat into gear, the whistle shrieking all the while.

Demitrova was near the end of his strength. He stopped swimming and tried to tread water, but a massive wave shoved him under. He came up slowly this time, head thrown back in exhaustion, just as the shark zeroed in on its quarry and turned to make a killing pass.

Sam's boat roared alongside him. Sam cut the throttle and seized a boat hook. As the shark made for Dimitri, Sam leaned far out, the boat hook held like a harpoon, and stabbed the animal with all his strength in its eye. The shark thrashed its head in pain and veered off. It finned a short distance away, only to turn and line up again, ready for another attack.

"Help!" Demitrova reached out with the last of his strength. Sam threw down the boat hook so he could reach overboard and latch onto Dimitri's uplifted arm just as a wave carried him under again. Demitrova clamped his hand around Sam's wrist and hung on with the desperate strength of a doomed man.

Sam kept his eye on the shark. He waited until the boat rocked on the top of a wave, and timing it right, with one mighty heave, yanked Dimitri Demitrova from the water and up onto the gunnel. Just below Demitrova's dangling feet, the pain-maddened, half-blind shark flashed by with a wide-open mouth and obscenely bared teeth. Sam heaved again, and this time both men splattered to the deck backwards, where Demitrova collapsed shaking and gasping.

The men lay there for several seconds before Sam disentangled himself and helped Demitrova to sit upright. He went to the cabin for a wool blanket and wrapped it snugly around Demitrova's naked, wet body. Sam could feel the man as he shivered violently. It was, Sam knew, a mixture of exhaustion, fear, cold, and relief.

Sam swiftly looked the man over, checking for injury and for blood. "Are you hurt, Dimitri? Can you get up?" Sam asked.

Demitrova shook his head and laughed wildly, hysterically. "I'm all right. I'm alive, Samuel! I'm alive!"

Sam helped Demitrova gain his feet, then went back again to the pilothouse. He returned with a pair of sweats, worn sneakers, and an old canvas jacket. He handed them to Demitrova.

"Here. Put these on," Sam commanded.

As Demitrova dressed, the two men took the time to look at each other.

"You actually came," Demitrova said with a touch of wonder in his voice as he buttoned the warm jacket all the way to his throat.

Sam handed him a canteen of water. "Amigo, you took one hell of a chance if you ever doubted that."

Demitrova guzzled the water in a long, grateful draught, took another gulp, and paused to catch his breath. "One way or the other, I was leaving that place. I told you that, Samuel."

"So you did. I wasn't always sure of that—but they certainly will be on the island."

Demitrova chuckled. "I left my clothes on the dock, along with a note—a last goodbye. A 'see you in Hell' letter addressed to Samuel Ransom Spears."

Sam laughed. "That *is* a good touch. Now, come. Give me a hand. We have a lot to do and no time to waste."

The men went to the transom and hauled the sailboat into position alongside. Then they retrieved the footlocker and a duffel bag from the cabin of Sam's boat and transferred them to the cockpit of the sailboat.

Up above, the moon was almost full again. Sam handed Demitrova his haversack and the wallet he had prepared back in his office.

"In the bag you'll find food, a pocketknife, towel, soap, toothbrush, and shaving gear. In the wallet, there are money and identity papers in the name of a merchant seaman from Malta. There are also four stamps and half a playing card.

"From here until you're out of Panamanian waters, travel only at night. There's a Russian trawler lurking just south of the islands, and I'm sure you don't want to bump into those boys. Head down the coast to Ecuador, to the port of Guayaquil. Once there, sink the boat and go ashore. Make your way to Quito, to the national university, and seek out Professor Carmelo Diaz. He is an old friend. Present him with your half of the card; he will show you the matching half.

"Professor Diaz will help you get settled. If you run out of money and need more, sell one of the stamps. The professor will tell you how. Live quietly and lie low. I'll get in touch with you as soon as I can. In an emergency, go to the professor; he'll know how to contact me. If, at any point, you feel you must flee, go to Iquitos in Peru. Find the bar El Chino and let yourself be seen there. That's where I'll find you. Is that clear? Any questions?"

"Yes, is all clear," Demitrova responded. "But Samuel, what if you must flee? What happens then?"

Sam was puzzled. "What?"

"Yes. What if you must flee? By helping me escape you have crossed a great divide, Samuel. What if at some point *you* must run? If they come for you, Samuel, what will *you* do?"

Sam shook his head firmly. "No one knows of this—will know of this, Dimitri. You've threatened suicide before. They will think you finally did it, that you swam out to sea and the sharks took you."

"I am talking about you now—you and your people, Samuel. There is a traitor in your organization. That's what Gottlieb and the others are looking for: the name of the traitor. That's what those men were killed for: the name of the Soviet double agent hidden in your midst. And they want—not to expose him—but to protect him from discovery."

"That's absurd beyond words," Sam retorted. But there was little conviction in the sound of his voice.

Demitrova went on with a rush. "He is in Washington, in your headquarters, Samuel. He passes his material through another agent in the British embassy."

"You know this for a fact?" Sam pressed.

Demitrova waved a hand. "I have heard. Others have heard too. Rumors. Boasting within Soviet Secret Service. But rumors can kill a man, Samuel; they have killed others already. And I believe these rumors are true."

Sam glanced up. The moon was now full again. "Maybe you're right, Dimitri. I don't know. Here, the night is burning; let's get your boat ready to sail."

The men worked together to quickly raise the jib and then the mainsail. As Sam hoisted the mizzensail, Demitrova went to man the tiller. Then Sam climbed over into his boat and untied the lines that held the two vessels together. Sam pitched Demitrova the lines, and the boats began to drift apart.

"A heading of one hundred fifteen degrees will take you to Piñas Bay. You should be there by daylight. Go to the mouth of the river and tie up under the trees until nightfall. Then sail on. There are charts in the locker for the journey, along with food and water. You'll also find a shotgun with a box of shells. And here—take this." Sam reached to his belt and tossed over his pistol. "You'll need this when you get ashore."

"One last thing, Samuel," Demitrova said as the boats drifted away from one another.

"Yes? What's that?"

"The night Kutasov died, I saw a man leaving his room."

"Leaving his room? Who?" Sam asked with surprise.

"A guard."

"Guard? Which guard?"

"I don't know. I caught only a glimpse from the back. But he was in guard uniform. He had on a white smock, but he wore khaki pants and boots. Only guards wear khaki and boots."

Sam stared fixedly at Demitrova but made no reply. He could think of nothing to say.

Demitrova called out more loudly now as the boats drifted farther apart. "Be very careful, Samuel. These are dangerous waters. You swim with sharks."

Sam raised a hand. "Go now. And go well, my friend."

Demitrova lifted his hand in return. "Adieu, Samuel Spears."

"Adios, Dimitri Demitrova."

Demitrova turned the tiller so that the sails caught the wind. There was a momentary pause as the sailboat found its head. Then the sails filled with a loud pop and the boat heeled over and sprang forward like a living creature.

Sam watched as Dimitri Demitrova sailed away under the full light of the moon. He then went to the helm and throttled up the engine. He watched Demitrova a bit longer as the sailboat made rapid progress, and then turning the wheel in the opposite direction, Sam motored off into the night.

* * * *

On the Contadora dock, Nolan Turner and Connor Sims stood looking at the pile of Demitrova's clothing. Just as the sun peeked over the mountains on the mainland, Turner lifted the bottle and spied the edge of a piece of paper sticking out of the shirt pocket. He opened the paper and began to read. He then turned to Sims and said, "Go tell Mr. Driscoll we have a problem."

"What is it? What's the problem?" asked Sims with a frown.

Turner looked out to sea and smiled ruefully as he put the note in his pocket. "Well, for starters, there will be one less for breakfast."

* * * *

Sam motored into Diablo Landing just as the sun climbed above the treetops. He ran a hand across the stubbled whiskers of his face and blinked a reddened eye that felt as if it were filled with sand.

The trip back in had taken five hours. Five hours that felt like ten because they'd all been spent pounding directly into the wind and the waves. He was sodden with salt spray. His mind and body were fatigued. His legs felt rubbery and unsure as he tied up at the dock. The boat now secure, he took his cane in hand and, with a pronounced limp, trudged wearily to his car. Times like these made Sam glad he had his walking stick at hand.

As Sam neared his car, his primal, almost animal-like sixth sense kicked in. He felt a physical tingle that flipped a mental alert, and his tiredness was gone just like that. He had been watching the ground. He looked up and into the eyes of two masked men, each with a machete in hand, as they stepped from the cover of an old abandoned warehouse.

Sam stopped dead in his tracks. He glared at the men and knew immediately what this meant. And just as suddenly, he felt explosive, raging anger fill him and rip joyfully, musically through his body.

As the battle madness took charge of his being, Sam felt godlike and utterly powerful. The only thing that had any meaning to him at all, no matter whether he lived or died, was to kill his enemy.

Sam ripped the eye patch from his head and flung it to the ground. He stamped on it with his good leg and roared, "Que carajo, pendejos! You cuecos need machetes for a one-eyed cripple with a cane?"

The men stared in stunned disbelief at the black, empty eye socket of Sam's maniacal, hate-filled face. They hesitated. One of the men took a step backward.

Sam lifted his cane in a fighting stance. He dripped scorn when he flung the foulest insult in the Spanish language full into their faces: "Yo caigo! Yo caigo en la leche de tu puta madre!"

He took a step forward and screamed, more enraged, "Adelante coños!"

The men raised their machetes and Sam crouched for the attack. But at that instant, a rope was thrown around Sam's neck from behind and he was yanked violently backward.

With no hesitation—for hesitation would be fatal—Sam leapt upward, his feet clearing the ground a good foot. While in the air, Sam whipped the cane around and behind the neck of his would-be strangler. He grabbed the other end of the cane, trapping the man's neck, and yanked forward, pinning his head onto Sam's shoulder.

As his feet touched the ground, Sam bent forward and crashed to his knees, hurling his attacker over his shoulders in a high arc and sending him sailing through the air. The man spun in the air and crashed to the ground on his back, his breath knocked out of his lungs with a loud *whoosh*!

Sam spun his cane around in his hand and delivered a lightning blow with the heavy knob end, shattering the man's nose. In less than a blink, he slammed in two more blows, driving bone splinters deep into the man's brain, killing him instantly.

The masked men with machetes were stunned frozen by the ferocity of Sam's murderous counterattack. It was all the advantage Sam needed. He hurled himself at the nearest one, viciously slashing his cane down on the man's wrist and breaking the bones with a loud, sickening wet *snap.* The machete fell clattering to the ground as the man clutched his broken wrist and pressed it to his chest, reeling away and yowling in excruciating pain.

The other assailant launched his assault and a desperate, swirling fight ensued, wooden cane against machete. The masked attacker came on with wild slashes of his long blade. Sam spun on his good leg, letting the weight of his other leg act as a counterbalance to his movements.

Sam sidestepped a wild overhand blow that came whistling by his ear. As the man's weight and momentum carried him past, Sam spun on his toe and landed a heavy blow against the back of the man's neck. The man fell to a knee but got back up and turned to face Sam again. He paused, breathing heavily, to size Sam up for his next attack.

The man with the broken right wrist now returned to pick up his machete and rejoin the fight. He held the machete awkwardly in his left hand and flourished it feebly, but it meant Sam had to fight again on two fronts.

Sam parried a blow from the main attacker; then, spotting an opening, he shot forward with a lightning thrust and stabbed the man with the broken wrist directly in the throat with the tip end of the cane. The man dropped to his knees, his larynx crushed. He fell onto his side, thrashing in agony, choking to death.

Sam immediately turned and lunged at the last man as he stood staring at his dying comrade. Sam slashed at the machete hand but the man deftly spun on his heel and stepped back, taking the blow on his other arm. He countered with a machete slash, but Sam parried and whirled his cane in a full circle, this time striking the man on the side of the head just above the temple. The man staggered a step but quickly recovered and came back again.

Sam barely turned a powerful backhanded stroke that whistled within a hair's breadth of his face. As the attacker's momentum carried him forward, Sam jumped to one side and planted a kick on the man's knee, knocking him off balance. It gave him just the opportunity he needed. Sam landed a sickening blow on the man's elbow, making him drop the machete and stumble back a step. Sam kicked the machete aside and stood erect. He gestured to the man with his cane.

"Bastante? Enough?" Sam asked, his chest laboring as he tried to catch his breath.

In reply, the man grinned. He reached calmly to his hip and brought out a pistol. He flipped off the safety and took deliberate aim at the center of Sam's chest.

Sam dropped like a shot to a crouch and hurled his cane at the man's face. He launched himself at the man full force, his body sailing through the air like a thrown spear. The man threw a hand to his face to ward off the cane just as Sam's head struck him in the solar plexus.

The two men crashed to the ground as the pistol went off with an ear-shattering roar. Sam came up atop the man, straddling his chest. He clamped one hand on the man's throat and drew back his arm to land a killing blow.

But he stopped, his fist hanging in the air. And stared at the neat black hole in the man's left temple. The right side of the man's head was blown away, scattered across the dirt in ragged shards of bone and gobs of pink and white goo. Blood puddled beneath the man's ruined head as his legs kicked spastically and his feet drummed the ground in his final death throes.

Sam swung off the body and onto both knees, his hands on his thighs for support as he gasped for breath and trembled from the violent exertion of combat. He heaved up to see Cholo stepping forward and kicking the pistol away before he fired two more shots into the carcass on the ground.

Sam rested on his knees with his head down, panting and exhausted. Cholo gave him a minute and then touched him on the shoulder. Then he helped Sam to his feet. He looked around until he spotted Sam's cane and then brought it to him.

"Estás herido?" Cholo asked as he checked Sam gently for wounds.

Sam's jacket was cut in several places and the knees of his trousers were torn, but other than a graze across his left forearm from the machete, he was unharmed.

Sam looked down, ran a hand over his body and then shook his head. "No. I'm okay."

Cholo picked up Sam's eye patch and handed it to him. Sam slapped the patch against his leg to knock the sand loose and put it back in place.

"Gracias, hermano," he said, looking around the scene of combat and at the bodies of the dead men crumbled and bleeding across the ground. He was bone tired.

"Who the hell are they?" he asked.

Cholo reached down and pulled the masks off the first two men Sam had dispatched.

"No los conozco. No son de Villanueva."

Sam realized that both he and Cholo had been expecting to see Villanueva's men, but these two had the look of street thugs—men who could be hired for a few dollars to administer a beating or cut a throat.

"I don't know them either," Sam said. He leaned down and pulled the mask from the last body, the man Cholo had shot.

"I'll be damned! Dimitri, you were right after all," Sam said as he and Cholo stared down at the body of Alton Chambers.

Moffitt tried to warn me and Chambers killed him for it. But Chambers wasn't a thinker or a planner—he was a field soldier. So who was he working for? Someone on the island or someone else? Was he the one talking to the Russian trawler, or was there an intermediary in the city? How big is the conspiracy? Who's in on it? And how far up does it reach?

Sam looked around the area, at the deserted dock and the abandoned warehouses that blocked the view and access to this secluded stretch of waterfront.

At least no one knows what happened here. There are no witnesses. If anyone else were involved they would be here to make sure I was dead. So I have time and a chance. Clean this mess up and act like nothing ever happened. Continue the hunt for Chambers—the missing guard. Someone will get curious when he doesn't report and they'll follow up. That's when they'll show their hand and that's when I'll know for certain who else is involved. But what to do about it, I don't know, because I don't know who I can trust. I don't even know if I can trust Carleton with this.

Sam felt very alone but knew that he wasn't. He looked at his friend and compañero Cholo Martinez, the one man he knew he could trust—and trusted with his life. Sam motioned to the bodies on the ground.

"Come on. Let's get this carrion aboard the boat before the buzzards begin to circle. Sharks gotta eat too you know."

The two men sweated and struggled as they loaded the dead bodies onto the boat. Then Cholo went to his jeep and brought back a shovel. He scooped up the scattered bits of Chambers' head and blood-sodden soil and tossed them in the water. Sam went along behind, kicking sand over the places where the gore had puddled. Then he did a quick search of the area for the four empty cartridge cases and put those carefully in his pocket.

The cleanup finished, the men hurriedly climbed aboard the boat. Cholo cast off lines as Sam stepped to the helm and cranked the engine. Cholo draped a tarp over the stack of bodies as they pulled away from the dock and then came to stand with Sam.

As they got underway, Sam looked over at his friend and said, "You know, there's one thing that puzzles me, Cholo."

"Si? Digame," replied Cholo before reaching over the gunnel to splash water on a bloodied hand.

"How did you know? How did you know to be here?" Sam asked.

Cholo dried his hand on his pants. "Major Rivera—Jesús. He call me. He tell me to be here. He tell me you gonna need help."

Sam grinned. Then he threw his head back and laughed aloud for what seemed the first time in weeks. He looked Cholo in the eye and grinned widely. "Well, hermano mio, I guess it's true what we've always been told."

Cholo wrinkled his brow in confusion and looked at Sam as if he had turned gringo on him all of a sudden. "Verdad? Qué es verdad?"

Sam steered the boat into the shipping channel and headed them out to sea. He reached in his pocket for the cartridge cases, started to toss them overboard, but giving them a quick glance placed them back again in his pocket. Only then did Sam turn to Cholo and reply in a solemn voice but with a devilish gleam in his eye, "Jesús saves."

Cholo held Sam's look a second then shrugged and turned to watch a passing ship. He said nothing in response, because sometimes, like now, he had no idea what the hell his friend was talking about.